Camp Club Girls

Kate and the
WYOMING FOSSIL
FIASCO

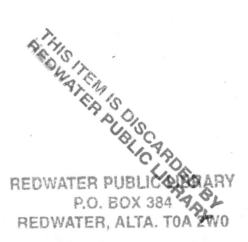

To Calyn Hazeltine. . .a priceless treasure

© 2011 by Barbour Publishing, Inc.

Edited by Jeanette Littleton.

ISBN 978-1-60260-405-6

Scripture quotations are taken from the King James Version of the Bible.

Scripture taken from the New King James Version®. Copyright © 1982 by Thomas Nelson, Inc. Used by permission. All rights reserved.

This book is a work of fiction. Names, characters, places, and incidents are either products of the author's imagination or used fictitiously. Any similarity to actual people, organizations, and/or events is purely coincidental.

Cover design: Thinkpen Design

Published by Barbour Publishing, Inc., P.O. Box 719, Uhrichsville, Ohio 44683, www.barbourbooks.com

Our mission is to publish and distribute inspirational products offering exceptional value and biblical encouragement to the masses.

Member of the
Evangelical Christian
Publishers Association

Printed in the United States of America.

Dickinson Press Inc., Grand Rapids, MI 49512; February 2011; D10002688

Camp Club Girls

Kate and the
WYOMING FOSSIL
FIASCO

Janice Hanna

BARBOUR
PUBLISHING

CHAPTER 1

Water, Water Everywhere!

"Kate, watch out!"

Kate Oliver jerked her arm back as she heard her teacher's voice.

Kaboosh! A large glass of water tumbled over, landing directly on the fossil plate she had just unpacked from a large wooden box.

"Oh no!" Kate squeezed her eyes shut. Surely she did *not* just spill water on a priceless artifact, thousands of years old!

"Quick. Let me dry it." Mrs. Smith, Kate's teacher, grabbed a paper towel and ran toward Kate.

Kate backed away, shaking so hard her knees knocked. "I–I'm so sorry! I didn't mean to spill it."

Of all things! She had come to the museum to help her teacher. And now she'd destroyed something of great value! Why oh why did things like this always seem to happen to her?

"It's not your fault, Kate," Mrs. Smith said. "I left my glass of water sitting there. I only have myself to blame."

"Still. . ." Kate's glasses slipped down her nose, and she pushed them back into place. Tears filled her eyes as she watched her teacher. How would the museum ever replace something so valuable? And would Mrs. Smith lose her new job as museum curator? A shiver ran down the twelve-year-old's spine.

"Please, Lord, don't let that happen!" she whispered.

"Wait a minute. . ." Mrs. Smith shook her head as she dabbed the fossil plate with the paper towel. "Something is very wrong here."

Kate leaned forward to look. "W—what is it?"

"A glass of water couldn't possibly harm *real* fossils," Mrs. Smith explained. "But look at this." She pulled the towel away and Kate gasped. The fossil imprint appeared to be dissolving, slowly melting away before her eyes.

"I don't understand." Kate took her finger and twisted a strand of her blond hair, something she often did when she was nervous.

"Neither do I," Mrs. Smith said as she pulled off her latex gloves. "But I'm going to get to the bottom of this." When her hands were free of the gloves, she pulled out a magnifying glass and examined the fossil plate. After a moment, she whispered, "Oh my. This doesn't look good."

Kate grew more curious by the moment.

"Kate, see what you think." Mrs. Smith handed her the magnifying glass. Kate peered through it, taking a close look.

"Very interesting," she said. "They look like grains of

sand, only maybe a little bigger."

Kate reached into her backpack and pulled out a miniature digital camera, just one of her many electronic gadgets. She zoomed in and began taking photos, documenting the changes in the fossil as they occurred. She had a feeling these photos would come in handy later.

"Up close it doesn't even look real. Funny that I never noticed it before." Mrs. Smith touched a spot where the water had landed, then stuck her finger in her mouth. Her eyes grew wide as she looked at Kate. "You've got to be kidding me!"

"What?" Kate asked. "What is it?"

Her teacher gasped. "Brown sugar!"

"No way!" Kate took one final picture of Mrs. Smith with her finger in her mouth. "The fossil plates are. . .fake?"

"Looks that way." Her teacher put down the magnifying glass and shook her head. "I don't believe it. I simply don't believe it. These plates are on loan to the museum from a quarry in Wyoming. We're expecting hundreds of guests to visit the museum to see them. And now we find out they're not even real? This is terrible news!" She reached for a piece of paper and began to fan herself. "Is it getting hot in here?"

Kate shook her head. "Not really." She put her camera away and then looked at her teacher, trying to figure out how she could help.

"I must be nervous." Mrs. Smith paced the room. "What am I going to do?"

She paused and looked at Kate. "This exhibition was supposed to be the biggest thing to happen to our museum in years. People were coming from all over the country to see these fossils. Oh, why does something like this have to happen my first week as curator? Why?"

"I don't know, but I would sure like to get to the bottom of this," Kate said. "So if you don't mind. . ." She pressed her hand inside the backpack, fishing around for something. Finally she came up with the tiny fingerprint kit.

Mrs. Smith looked at her, stunned. "You just *happen* to have a fingerprint kit in your backpack?"

"Yes." Kate giggled. "I always carry it with me. I never know when there's going to be a mystery to solve or a criminal to catch."

"You solve mysteries?" Mrs. Smith looked confused. "And you catch criminals?"

Kate nodded and smiled, "Along with a bunch of others called the Camp Club Girls."

She would have plenty of time to explain later. Right now she had work to do. She pulled out several other gadgets, starting with a tiny digital recorder. "I'd like to record our conversation, Mrs. Smith. You might say something important to the case."

"Case?"

"Sure. I have a feeling this is going to be a very exciting one, but I need to keep track of the information, and recording it is the best way."

"I suppose that would be fine." Mrs. Smith shrugged.

Kate turned on the recorder and set it on a nearby table, asking her teacher questions about the fossil plates. Then she pulled something that looked like an ink pen from her backpack.

Mrs. Smith looked at her curiously. "Do you need to write something?"

"No, this isn't really a pen." Kate wiggled her eyebrows and smiled. "It's a text reader. Look." She took the pen-like device and ran it along the edge of the wooden box the fossil plates had been packed in. It recorded the words STONE'S THROW QUARRY, WYOMING'S FOSSIL FANTASY LAND.

"Very clever," Mrs. Smith said with a nod.

After recording a few more words from the side of the box, Kate turned her attention back to her backpack. She pulled out the computerized wristwatch her father had given her. One of his students had invented it, and soon it would be sold in stores. She could hardly believe it was possible to check her e-mail or browse the Web on a wristwatch, but it had already come in handy several times.

Her teacher looked at Kate's gadgets, her brow wrinkling in confusion. "Why do you have all of these things, Kate? Do you really solve mysteries, or is this some sort of game?"

Kate shook her head. "It's no game. And it looks like we have a doozy of a mystery here. But to solve it, I need to contact the other Camp Club Girls."

"Camp Club Girls? I'm not sure I understand. Who are the Camp Club Girls?"

"We're a group of girls who all met at Discovery Lake Camp awhile back," Kate explained. "We solve mysteries together. If anyone can get to the bottom of this, the Camp Club Girls can."

Mrs. Smith's eyes grew wide. "Really? Do you think you could help figure out who did this? That's a lot to ask of a group of girls your age."

"You would be surprised what the Camp Club Girls can do with the Lord's help!" Kate went to work, lifting fingerprints from the edges of the fossil plate. Before long, she had a couple of great ones. "Perfect. Now, if it's okay with you, I need to send an e-mail to the girls in the club to see if they can help."

"Well sure," Mrs. Smith said. "I guess that would be okay. Do you need to use one of the museum's computers to get online? I'm sure I could arrange that."

"No thanks." Kate pulled off her latex gloves and opened her wristwatch. "I can send e-mails on my watch."

"You. . .you can?" Mrs. Smith did not look convinced.

Kate typed out a quick note to the girls:

Emergency! Need help cracking a fake fossil case!
Meet me in our chat room at 7:00 p.m. eastern time.

She closed the watch and smiled at her teacher. "Don't

worry, Mrs. Smith," she said, trying to sound brave. "The Camp Club Girls are on the case! We'll figure out this fossil fiasco in no time!"

With the tip of her finger, she reached to touch the ruined fossil plate then stuck her finger in her mouth, tasting the sweetness of the brown sugar. These plates might not be the real deal, but they sure were tasty. And Kate was convinced they contained clues to help unravel the mystery.

Suddenly, she could hardly wait to get started!

A Sweet Adventure

The fossil fiasco gave Kate and the Camp Club Girls an exciting new puzzle to solve. She could hardly wait! Surely, with the Lord's help, they would crack this case wide open! She thought about this all the way home from the museum.

As Kate ate dinner with her parents that evening, she filled them in on what had happened. "I felt terrible when I spilled the water," she said. "But Mrs. Smith said it wasn't my fault."

"I'm sure she felt awful for leaving her glass so close to the fossil plates," Kate's mother said. "I guess it just goes to show you how careful you have to be around things of value."

"But look on the bright side, Kate," her father added. "If you hadn't spilled water on them, she might have never discovered they were fake. The whole thing could have been a huge embarrassment to your teacher if the exhibition had moved forward and someone discovered the forgery after the fact. People who paid money to see the fossils would have been angry to find out they'd been lied to. So you probably saved the day, whether you realize it or not."

"I never thought of that!" Kate suddenly felt better. "I guess it's a good thing we found out now instead of later." She took a couple of bites of mashed potatoes, then leaned back in her chair, thinking about her father's words. Maybe spilling that water *had* saved the day, after all.

Her little brother Dexter took a bite of meatloaf, then talked with his mouth full. "Kate, can I help you and the Camp Club Girls with this case?"

She shrugged. "Probably, Dex. But I need to talk to the other girls." Kate glanced at the wall clock, startled to find it was fifteen minutes till seven.

Her dad changed the topic of conversation, talking about the family's upcoming vacation to Colorado, but Kate had a hard time paying attention. She only had one thing on her mind right now. . .getting online to meet the other Camp Club Girls in their Internet chat room.

A few minutes later, after eating a second helping of meatloaf and mashed potatoes, Kate headed upstairs. She glanced at her reflection in the large round mirror that hung on the wall. Her shoulder-length blond hair was a little messy, but she didn't really mind. After all, she couldn't be a supersleuth and have perfect hair at the same time, could she? Still, she needed to do something about her glasses, which had slipped down her nose again. Kate pushed them back up with her finger and shrugged.

"C'mon, Biscuit!" She looked down at her dog. His tail

waved merrily as he followed her up the stairs. Biscuit could always tell when they were about to set off on an adventure. He was a great mystery-solving dog and had even helped the girls before. Maybe he could help this time, too.

When she reached the top of the stairs, Kate turned to walk down the long hall toward her bedroom and almost tripped over Robby, the robovac. As always, Biscuit barked at the little robotic vacuum cleaner and Kate scolded him. "I would think by now you would be used to Robby, Biscuit! Stop barking."

The pooch tucked his tail between his legs and followed her to her bedroom. Once there, Kate grabbed her new laptop—the one her father had given her. It was super-duper fast and Kate was so thankful that it had wireless Internet connection so she could use it anywhere in the house. Kate signed online, realizing the other Camp Club Girls were waiting for her in the chat room—Bailey, the youngest, twelve-year-old Sydney, and Elizabeth, the oldest of the girls. Somehow, knowing they were on the case made everything better.

> Kate: *K8 here. Everyone else here?*
> Sydney: *I'm here.*
> Bailey: *So am I! Ready for adventure!*
> Elizabeth: *I really want to help. Just tell me what I can do.*
> Alexis: *Yes, this sounds really curious. But we*

need to know more before we can help you.
McKenzie: *Kate, can you tell us more about
the fake fossils? Your e-mail didn't have much
information.*

Kate quickly explained what had happened at the
museum, typing as fast as her fingers could go. She told
them every detail—about the accident with the water, the
fake fossils, and her teacher's fears that she might lose her
new job.

Kate: *I think we can start by figuring out where
Stone's Throw Quarry is. I saw the name on the
packing crates. That's where the fossils are from.*
McKenzie: *Ooh, hang on a minute. I think I'm on
to something. There's a Stone's Throw Quarry
south of Yellowstone National Park, just a few
hours from where I live. I'm looking at their
Web site now.*

Seconds later, she pasted in the link and before long
Kate clicked it, watching as the colorful site appeared.

Kate: *Wow. Looks like a great place. This is cool.
Stone's Throw hosts a three-day fossil camp
for kids, week after next. I wonder. . . Our
family is supposed to leave in a couple of*

*days to go on a trip to Rocky Mountain
National Park in Colorado. Maybe I could talk
my mom and dad into driving up to Yellowstone National Park afterwards so I could go to
that fossil camp. They could set up their tent at
the park and McKenzie and I could go to the
camp hosted by the quarry. I'll bet if we spent
a few days there, I could take some fingerprints and compare them to the ones I got
today. Maybe we could figure out who
forged the fossils!*

Bailey: *Forged the fossils. That's funny.*

Kate: *If we don't figure this out, Mrs. Smith could
lose her new job at the museum. And the
museum will lose a lot of visitors. We've got
to find the real fossils and get them to the
museum in time for the exhibition.*

McKenzie: *I would love to help. I'll have to ask
my parents of course. Maybe they would
like to go to Yellowstone, too. It's one of
my dad's favorite places and he's been talking
about going on a vacation soon.*

Kate: *Great! Just pray that my mom and dad like
the idea.*

She tucked a loose blond hair behind her ear.
"That your mom and dad like *what* idea?" Her

mother's voice rang out from behind her.

Kate turned and faced her mom with an embarrassed smile. "Oh hi, Mom."

"Hi to you, too. What have you and the other girls come up with, and how does the plan involve your father and me?"

"Oh, it's the best idea ever," Kate said, giving her mom a hopeful smile. "I need to go to a fossil hunting camp in Wyoming week after next."

"Wyoming?" Her mother stared at her, looking a little stunned. "But we're not going to Wyoming. We're going to Colorado."

Kate flashed another smile, hoping to convince her mom. "Think about it. Wyoming would be a great place to visit. You and Dad can camp out at Yellowstone National Park with Dex while I'm at fossil camp. I know how much you've always wanted to do that."

"Honey, we're going to *Rocky Mountain* National Park in Colorado," her mother explained. "Not Yellowstone."

"Can't we do both?" Kate asked. "Please? Oh please?"

"Kate, you don't seriously think. . ." Her mother shook her head. "Oh never mind. I can see that you *do* think we might consider this." After a pause, she said, "Well I promise to talk to your father about it. But don't get your hopes up. I'm not sure your father will like the idea. It's a long drive from Rocky Mountain National Park to Yellowstone."

"But it will be so worth it if I can help my teacher figure

out who did this," Kate said. "Besides, it would be a great adventure. And I know Dex would love it." She smiled as she mentioned her little brother's name. Just as quickly, her smile disappeared as she realized he would probably want to go to the quarry camp, too. How could the girls ever solve a mystery with her little brother tagging along?

Kate's mother left the room, and Kate realized the girls had gone on chatting without her. She skimmed their posts, getting caught up.

McKenzie: *This is what we'll do. K8 and I will go to the camp and figure out who would want to forge a fossil and why.*

Sydney: *And the rest of us will help, too! We'll figure this out!*

Bailey: *I wish I could go to fossil camp with you! But I know my mom won't let me.*

Alexis: *This whole thing reminds me of a documentary I saw last year with my dad. I'm going to watch it again. Maybe it will give us some clues.*

Sydney: *I'm going to research the quarry online before you get there. So call me, okay?*

Kate: *Okay.*

Elizabeth: *This reminds me a little of the story of Jacob and Esau from the Old Testament. Do you remember that one? Jacob pretended to be his brother Esau so that he could steal his birthright. He put on animal*

*skins to try to fool his dad into thinking he was really
his brother.*

Kate: *Oh that's right. And his dad, Isaac, fell for it,
didn't he?*

Elizabeth: *Yes. Sometimes pretenders get away with
things. A lot of people are really good at faking it.*

McKenzie: *Some aren't so good. That's why we have to
figure this out!*

Elizabeth: *I'm going to read that story again tonight.
And I will pray. Maybe the Lord will drop some clues
in our lap and we can solve this case.*

Kate: *I'll be in touch. We'll figure this out!*

Bailey: *Yes, send us text messages. Or call.*

Kate: *Maybe we'll have wireless Internet access, too. But
we'll stay in touch, I promise. Now pray that my
parents say yes.*

The girls said their good-byes and Kate signed off-line.
Then she curled up on the bed with Biscuit at her side. She
hugged him. "What do you think, Wonder Dog? Are you
ready for a fossil-tastic adventure?"

He reached up to lick her face and she giggled. Looked
like Biscuit was ready to go! Now if only her parents would
join the fun!

CHAPTER 3

Kate Goes to Yellowstone

Just a week and a half after the fossil fiasco, Kate's father drove the family's van to the entrance of Yellowstone National Park. He had agreed that after a week in Colorado, the Oliver clan would go to Wyoming so Kate could go to fossil camp. Talk about an answer to prayer!

As they entered the park, her father shook his head. "I still can't believe you talked me into this."

"But we'll have so much fun!" Kate gave him an encouraging smile.

"You're probably right." He steered their van toward the campsite. They arrived moments later and worked together to unload and set up the family's large tent.

"I want to go to fossil camp, too," Dexter grumbled. "It's not fair that Mom and Dad won't let me."

"Who knows? You may have an adventure of your own, here at Yellowstone," Kate said. Leaning closer, she whispered, "You know there are bears here, right?"

"Bears?" He reached for the video camera and held it up. "If I see one, I'll tape it! Maybe I'll make a movie to show my friends. I'll call it. . .Un-*bear*-able!"

Kate laughed until her sides hurt. Suddenly she didn't feel so bad about leaving Dexter here while she went to fossil camp.

An hour later, McKenzie's family arrived. Kate smiled as her friend climbed out of their large RV. She could hardly believe how much older McKenzie looked. At thirteen, McKenzie was the second oldest of the Camp Club Girls. She was much taller than last time.

McKenzie wore her red hair pulled back in a ponytail and freckles dotted her cheeks. The freckles were the only thing Kate and McKenzie had in common. Well, the only thing except their faith and their love of crime solving!

"It's so great to see you again!" McKenzie hugged Kate. Then she scratched Biscuit behind the ears. "And it's supergreat to see Biscuit, too. I've missed you, boy!"

He rolled over on his back, begging for his tummy to be rubbed.

"Okay, you silly thing." McKenzie laughed as she knelt to tickle his tummy. "I never could keep from spoiling you."

The happy pooch rolled in the dirt, glad to get so much attention.

"I'm so happy your parents agreed to come!" Kate said. "Can you believe we're really here?"

"No, but I'm so glad!" McKenzie looked up from tickling Biscuit's tummy and grinned. "Oh Kate, we'll have the best time in the world. Fossil camp. Can you believe we actually get to go?"

McKenzie's mother walked up. "I can't believe we let you girls talk us into this," she said.

After the Phillipses got settled in, the two families gathered around the campfire, where they roasted hot dogs and nibbled on potato chips. Kate ate her first hot dog then reached for another.

After eating hot dogs, they roasted marshmallows. Kate ate three in a row then smacked her lips. "Man! Those were good!"

"Tell us the whole story about why we've come to Wyoming, Kate," Mrs. Phillips said. "What happened with your teacher at the museum, and what are you and McKenzie hoping to find on your adventure at the quarry?"

Kate put down her stick. "Well, my science teacher, Mrs. Smith, just got a new job at the Museum of Natural Science in Philadelphia. She's a curator."

"What's a curator?" Dexter asked, looking up from his sticky marshmallow.

"A curator is the one in charge of the projects," Kate explained. "She organizes the collections. Mrs. Smith was organizing the new fossil collection and it turned out to be fake."

"Oh I see." Dexter swallowed the rest of his marshmallow, licked his fingers, and went back to playing with his Gameboy.

"Tell us again how you found out they were fake," Mrs. Phillips said.

"We were unpacking the fossils from their boxes when I accidentally spilled a glass of water on one of them," Kate explained.

Mr. Phillips shrugged. "A little water shouldn't hurt anything."

"That's just it," Kate said. "The imprint began to melt and Mrs. Smith realized the fossils weren't fossils at all. We looked closer and found out someone had forged them!"

"Out of sand?" Mr. Phillips asked. "I suppose that would be the obvious choice."

"No." Kate shook her head. "You'll never believe it. Brown sugar!"

"Oh my." Mrs. Phillips looked stunned. "Must be someone who really knows his or her fossils to disguise brown sugar that well."

"Yes, a real pro," Kate's father agreed. "I think you girls need to keep your eyes open for people who have worked at the quarry a long time. Maybe you will find your suspect that way."

"Maybe," Kate said. "Or maybe the bad guy—or girl—doesn't work at the quarry at all. Maybe it's someone on the outside."

"What makes you think that?" her mother asked.

"Sydney did some research and sent me a list of other quarries in Wyoming that compete with Stone's Throw."

"Oh I see," her mother said. "Could be a competitor, trying to make Stone's Throw look bad."

"Exactly." Kate nodded. "Sydney also sent me a bunch of information about the type of fossils found at Stone's Throw and where they're sold, so we have a lot of information to go on."

"That's why we have to go to the quarry," McKenzie said. "To figure all of this out."

"I just hope we can crack this case," Kate said. "I don't want Mrs. Smith to lose her job. I got an e-mail from her just yesterday. She said that the board members at the museum are holding a special meeting next week. Some of them are holding her responsible for this, but it's not her fault. She had no idea those fossils were fake until I spilled the water."

"Well of course she didn't. How could she?" McKenzie asked. "It's not like anyone goes around licking fossils or pouring water on them!"

"Still, we have to figure this out before that meeting," Kate explained. "If so, we can save the day."

"Remember, honey, only God can truly save the day." Kate's mother reached to give her a hug. "He uses us to touch others' lives, but ultimately only He can work the miracles, not us."

Kate nodded. "Thanks, Mom. Just keep praying, okay?"

"I will, honey."

"And we will do what we can to help, too," Mr. Phillips said. "Tomorrow, when we drop you off at the quarry for fossil camp, we'll go on the tour. Maybe we can unearth some helpful information." He laughed and then slapped his knee. "Get it? *Unearth* some helpful information?"

Kate giggled.

"I'm sure McKenzie will be a big help to you, Kate," Mrs. Phillips said. "She always has a way of digging deep to find answers."

"Digging deep! That's a good one!" Mr. Phillips slapped his knee again. "Man! We're on a roll, aren't we?"

Everyone had a good laugh. It made Kate feel terrific to know their parents were excited about this. Now, if only she and McKenzie and the other Camp Club Girls could actually solve this case in time for Mrs. Smith to keep her job. . .then all would be well!

CHAPTER 4

Fossil-tastic Fun!

The next morning, Kate's dad drove the girls to Stone's Throw Quarry, about an hour away from Yellowstone. Mr. Phillips went along for the ride. So did Dexter. Kate could hardly contain her excitement, not just about the camp, which started at ten o'clock, but about spending time with McKenzie, too. All along the way, she kept in touch with the other Camp Club Girls by sending text messages to keep them updated.

"Elizabeth says she's praying for us," Kate whispered to McKenzie.

"And Bailey says to have fun!" McKenzie added, looking up from her phone.

The girls giggled.

Just then, Kate received an e-mail on her wristwatch. She looked up at McKenzie, wide-eyed. "Sydney says to drink lots of water because we're at a higher elevation."

"Oooh, good idea." McKenzie nodded. "If anyone would know about that kind of stuff, Sydney would."

Kate typed a response to Sydney's e-mail then sent it.

"There. I told her we would use sunscreen and drink lots of water."

"Don't you just love technology?" Kate's father said. "Here we are, in the middle of Wyoming, and the girls can stay in touch with their friends all over the country by text messages or e-mails."

"Oh, that's nothing," Kate said. "Just wait till tonight! We're doing another Internet chat with our friends. It'll be great. They're all on the case."

"I love it." McKenzie's father smiled. "Back when we were their age, we didn't even have cell phones."

"You didn't?" Dexter looked at them, clearly stunned. "How did you talk to people?"

"Well for one thing, we spent a lot more time talking to the people we were actually with," Mr. Phillips said. "If we had an emergency while driving down the road, we would stop and use a pay phone."

"Pay phone?" Dexter shrugged. "What's that?"

Kate's father laughed. "Never mind, son. Just trust us when we say that times have changed."

Dexter crossed his arms and leaned against the seat with a sour look.

Kate glanced his way, concerned. "Everything okay, Dex?"

"I just wish I could go with you to camp. You and McKenzie are going to have a lot of fun solving mysteries."

"Maybe next time," Kate said. She didn't worry too much about her little brother. He would have a lot of fun at

Yellowstone. "Think of all the bears you're going to see," she whispered.

His eyes grew large.

When they arrived at the quarry, Kate looked around, surprised by what she saw. Or rather, what she *didn't* see. To their right she noticed a boring-looking building and to the left, a parking lot. "Doesn't look very exciting," she said. "Pretty dull looking, actually."

"Yeah." McKenzie bit her lip and shrugged. "Hope we didn't make a mistake in coming."

"Looks can be deceiving," Mr. Phillips said. "You might be surprised what you find hiding under rocks or bushes." His wiggled his eyebrows and the girls laughed.

They got out of the car and Kate looked at her watch. "Looks like we're right on time."

"And it looks like we have just enough time to get you girls settled in before going on the tour," Mr. Phillips said. He looked at Kate's dad. "Are you game?"

"I'd love to go on the tour before we drive back," Kate's father said with a nod. "I've been working on a project with my robotics students back in Pennsylvania, and a trip to the quarry would help me think more creatively."

The girls made their way to the building with their dads behind them. They followed the signs that read CAMPERS SIGN IN HERE. As they joined a long line of other campers, the boy in front of Kate turned to look at her.

"You here for camp?" he asked, nudging up his glasses with his finger.

"Yes." She nodded. "I'm Kate and this is McKenzie."

"I'm Joel." He gave them a nod, then raked his fingers through his dark, curly hair. "I come every summer. This is my favorite camp."

"You go to other camps, too?" she asked.

"Sure." He shrugged. "Math camp. Science camp. Band camp. But this is the best."

"Well this is our first time," McKenzie explained. "And we have a lot to learn."

"I see." His brow wrinkled. "Newcomers. Well, welcome. If you have any questions about fossils, ask me. I'm your guy."

"He's your guy all right," McKenzie whispered in Kate's ear. "Sounds like you two have a lot in common."

"W–what?" Kate could hardly believe McKenzie would say such a thing!

McKenzie winked then looked from one to the other. Kate's stomach fluttered. How embarrassing! She hoped Joel hadn't heard. Or Dexter! He would tease her nonstop if he thought she was interested in a boy!

"You're both very scientific," McKenzie whispered. "And I'll bet he would love your electronic gadgets."

Thankfully the line moved forward. Before long a young man with a nametag that read CONNER greeted them.

"Welcome, ladies! And you are. . . ?"

"I'm Kate Oliver and this is McKenzie Phillips," Kate said. "We're first-time campers."

"Welcome to the best fossil-tastic adventure ever!"

Conner said. "You girls are in for a real treat. Want me to help you get checked in?"

"Please," McKenzie said.

He gave them each a clipboard. "Just fill out these forms for me. You can turn them back in here at the desk when you're done."

Kate nodded and took the paperwork, which she filled out lickety-split. McKenzie took a little longer. When they finished, they returned to the desk and Kate's father paid her tuition. McKenzie's father paid for hers as well.

"What about the tour, Dad?" Dexter asked. "You promised we could go!"

"There's a tour starting in ten minutes," Conner said. "I'll be leading it."

"How long does it last?" McKenzie asked. "Do we have time to go with our dads before camp starts?"

"Yes, it's just a thirty-minute tour of the quarry, which is behind this building," Conner said. "When you're done, meet Megan at the bunkhouse, and she will get you settled in." He pointed to a pretty young woman in her twenties with blond hair and a bright smile.

She drew near. "Did someone call my name?"

"I was just telling our new campers to meet you at the bunkhouse after the tour," Conner said. "This is their first time at Stone's Throw."

"Welcome." Megan extended her hand and Kate shook it. "I'm Megan Jenkins."

"Megan's father, Mr. Jenkins, owns the quarry," Conner explained.

"That's right." Megan nodded. "I grew up just a couple of miles from here. Spent my childhood digging for fossils with my dad."

Kate smiled at the pretty blond. "I'm Kate Oliver and this is my friend McKenzie."

"We're glad you could join us at fossil camp," Megan said. "Enjoy the tour, and when you're done, I'll be at the bunkhouse to help you get settled in. We'll be great friends!"

"Thanks." Kate had a feeling she was right. They were going to be great friends.

The girls and their fathers walked to a sign with the words TOUR GROUPS on it. Then they went on the tour, which Conner led. They started by touring the museum. Kate noticed a room near the front that was open to the public, but another behind it said EMPLOYEES ONLY. Curiosity got the better of her. She tiptoed to the door, slipping away from the others on the tour. Unfortunately, it was locked. She wouldn't find out what was behind it. At least not today.

Next Conner led the way to the quarry's closest excavation site. He talked to the group about some great fossils that paleontologists had found there, and told them about a few that he had found as a teenager.

"I used to love to come here as a kid," he said. "There's just something about this place that really gets under your skin."

"Under your skin?" Dexter whispered, looking at his arms. "What does that mean?"

"He means once you come here you have to keep coming back. . .it's that much fun," McKenzie explained.

Dexter pouted.

Kate did her best to pay attention to Conner. He seemed like a great guy, and he certainly knew a lot about fossils! Maybe she could learn a few things from him.

When the tour ended, she hugged her father. "Dad, thanks so much for letting me come here. I'm going to have a blast."

"You're welcome, honey." He smiled down at her. "It looks like you'll be in good hands."

Both girls said their good-byes, and then headed to the bunkhouse to join Megan. She greeted them with a broad smile and a bubbly "Hello!" Once inside, she led them to their room, where three other campers were unloading their backpacks. Kate sized them up. The tall one with brown hair was probably twelve or thirteen. The short one with red hair and freckles was probably ten. And the one with the blond ponytail? She looked like the oldest of them all. . .maybe fifteen.

Megan quickly made the introductions. She pointed first to the girl with the blond ponytail. "Kate and McKenzie, I'd like you to meet Lauren." She gestured next to the blond. "This is Ginny." Finally she pointed to the cute little redhead. "And this is Patti."

Patti nodded. "Nice to meet you."

"Nice to meet you, too," Kate added. She couldn't help but smile. Meeting these girls reminded her of that day at Discovery Lake Camp when she first met McKenzie, Bailey, Elizabeth, and the others. Camp was always such a great place to make new friends.

After a few pleasant words, Kate and McKenzie started unloading their things.

"Did you bring everything on the list?" McKenzie asked, opening her backpack.

Kate went through the items, one by one. "I've got my sunscreen and sun hat. Comfy clothes. Sleeping bag and pillow. Backpack. Gloves. Hiking shoes. Toothbrush. Toothpaste. Shampoo." She looked at McKenzie. "Did I forget anything?"

"Yes!" Her friend looked shocked. "What about your gadgets?"

"Oh, I have all of those in this bag." Kate lifted her backpack where she'd put all of the good stuff—her laptop, the digital recorder, the text-reader pen, and much, much more. "I've got a GPS system on my phone in case we get lost," she said. "And I brought my laptop. I hope they let me use it." She looked at Megan, who flashed a smile.

"Sure. Those things are fine. We've got no problem with technology at fossil camp. In fact, the people who run the place encourage the campers to use all the technology they can to learn more while they're here. So Internet access is a plus."

Kate nodded. "Speaking of the Internet, we hoped to have a video chat with some friends tonight on my laptop." She gazed at Megan, more curious than ever. "Is that allowed?"

"As long as you do so before lights-out, it shouldn't be a problem," Megan said. "But trust me, if you girls get too rowdy after lights-out, that's a different story." She grinned. "I'm a pretty easygoing counselor, but I like my beauty sleep."

Kate laughed. Megan didn't look like she needed any beauty sleep. In fact, Kate couldn't help but hope she'd look like Megan when she got older.

"I brought lots of snacks, too!" Kate said, opening another, smaller bag. She dumped out dozens of candy bars, cookies, and chips.

Kate quickly ate a candy bar and tossed the wrapper in the trash. Then she put all the rest of her snacks away for later. In the meantime, she listened as McKenzie and Megan kept talking.

"Are you bunking in here with us?" McKenzie asked.

"Yes," Megan said. "And Conner bunks with the guys. If you need anything or have any questions, just ask."

"So what happens first?" McKenzie asked, glancing at her watch. "It's five after ten. Aren't we supposed to be doing something?"

"Conner is going to meet us at the excavation site at eleven o'clock," Megan said. "We'll give the campers some instructions before we break for lunch. There's a lot to learn before we begin."

"I'm sure!" Kate laughed. "I feel like I don't know anything about excavations!"

Lauren headed off with Ginny and Patti behind her. As they left their room, Kate glanced over and saw a Bible on Megan's bunk. She looked at her counselor with a smile. "Megan, you're a Christian?" she asked.

"I am." Megan flashed a broad smile. "You are, too?"

"Both of us," McKenzie said. "We met at a Christian camp awhile back."

"I'm so glad to hear this." Megan reached over and rested her hand on Kate's shoulder. "I always pray that the Lord will send just the right people to fossil camp. Looks like you're both here for a reason."

"Oh, we came to solve a mystery," Kate said. She quickly explained what had happened with the fake fossils, and Megan's eyes grew wide.

"You're saying the fossil plates that came from Stone's Throw were fake?" She paused then added, "I wonder if my dad already knows. He's been acting kind of down lately. This might explain it."

Kate nodded. "Our friends, the Camp Club Girls, are trying to figure out who would forge the fossils. . .and why. And I need to do it before my teacher loses her job!"

"Wow." Megan drew in a deep breath. "You really have a mystery on your hands, don't you." She paused once again. "But maybe the Lord has brought you here for more than that."

"What do you mean?" Kate asked.

"I mean a lot of kids come here to dig for fossils, but they end up digging for something else instead. Maybe there are some life lessons the Lord wants to teach you while you're here."

"Could be." McKenzie nodded.

"And who knows. . .maybe He wants you to do a little digging in His Word while you're here, too," Megan said with a twinkle in her eye. "Did you bring your Bibles with you?"

McKenzie nodded. "I did."

"I use an online Bible," Kate said. "I can read it on my phone or my laptop."

"Well, do this then," Megan said. "Every morning when you wake up, spend a little time digging in the Word before you pull out your chisel and dig in the rock. I have no doubt the Lord will reveal more than fossils to you while you're here."

"Good advice," McKenzie said.

"We'll do it!" Kate added.

Somehow the idea that the Lord had more in mind only made this adventure even more exciting.

Digging In

When the campers reached the excavation site, McKenzie glanced at Kate and grinned. "Look, there's that guy we met earlier." She nodded to Joel.

Kate looked at his jacket, hiking boots, and hard hat. "Man, he looks like he's ready to go. I can sure tell he's done this before."

"Looks like fun," McKenzie said. "And check out his backpack. It's huge. Must be loaded with equipment."

"Maybe he knows something we don't!" Kate mumbled. She looked at the rest of the campers, trying to size them up. Most were about her age. A couple were older though, including Joel.

He looked her way, smiled, and then stepped in her direction. "This is always my favorite part. . .listening to Conner and Megan explain about the tools and safety gear."

"You really *do* come here a lot," McKenzie said, looking puzzled. "You know everyone by name?"

He grinned. "Yeah. I want to be a paleontologist someday, so I've been coming to fossil camp every summer since I was ten."

Kate thought about his words for a moment. If he had been coming to the camp for several years, maybe he could help solve the mystery of the fake fossil plates. She asked, "How old are you now?"

"Fourteen." He paused. "Well, almost fourteen. My birthday isn't until September. But even after I'm too old for this camp, I'm going to keep coming because there's so much to learn. No matter how much I study, I always find out more when I come to camp. Fossils are so exciting."

Kate sighed. "I don't know anything about fossils."

"Me either," McKenzie said.

"Just hang out with me," Joel said as he grabbed his backpack.

"Yes, Joel is the person to learn from," Megan said, drawing near. "He's discovered some of the best fossils at the quarry over the past three years. If you want to see them, visit our display area."

"Really?" Kate stared at him with new appreciation. "So you're famous!"

His cheeks turned red. "Famous? No. But maybe someday I will be." He smiled in Conner's direction. "Like Conner. I want to be like him."

"You want to be like him?" Kate's eyes narrowed as she thought about this.

"Yes, he's the best here," Joel said with an admiring look on his face.

"Hey, what about me?" Megan pouted.

Joel grinned. "Sorry. You're great, too, Megan. It's just that Conner is so talented, and he's discovered some of the most valuable fossils on the property."

"It's true." Megan nodded. "Conner really knows his stuff, so if you girls have any questions I can't answer, I'll send you to him." She smiled. "But remember what I said about Joel. He knows almost as much as the counselors, so you might start by asking him your questions. And in case you didn't notice his stuff in the museum the day you arrived, you might look again."

Joel's cheeks turned even redder. "I'd love to help. Just let me know if you need anything."

"Thanks." Kate thought about that for a minute. Before long, suspicions set in. Perhaps Joel wasn't just a camper. Maybe he was a spy. She gazed at him, her eyes narrowing. Yes, maybe he had been sent from some other quarry to scope out the place. She would have to keep an eye on him over the next few days to see if he acted strange.

Conner joined the conversation. "Several paleontologists have taken an interest in Joel's work," he said. "Just ask Megan's father, who owns the quarry."

Megan nodded. "Some of the fossils Joel has found are really valuable. You can see them in the museum with his name next to them."

McKenzie's brow wrinkled. "But I thought we got to keep any fossils we found," she said. "Isn't that part of the purpose of this? To go home with real fossils?"

"Some you can keep and some you can't," Megan said. "It just depends on what you find."

"The fee we paid for the camp only allows us to collect common specimens," Joel explained. "If we discover something rare, it belongs to the state of Wyoming and has to stay here in the museum."

"Wow," Kate said. "I didn't know that."

He nodded. "That's right. And they take it very seriously. No one steals any fossils from Stone's Throw."

Kate wanted to say, "Oh yes they do!" but held her tongue. Surely someone here at Stone's Throw Quarry was stealing the real fossils and replacing them with fakes. But who? And why?

She didn't have much time to think about it. Conner called the group to the side of the hill and got everyone quieted down as he spoke.

"Welcome, everyone. In case you haven't already heard, my name is Conner Alexander and I'm a counselor here at Stone's Throw, as well as a paleontologist. I used to be a camper just like you." He grinned. "So, you never know, one day you might end up working here, too."

"I hope so," Joel whispered. "That's my goal."

"Hmm." Kate grew more suspicious than ever. Maybe Joel was just pretending to like Conner. Maybe he wanted to work here so he could steal the real fossils and replace them with fakes. She grew more nervous as she thought about it. Just as quickly, she scolded herself. *You don't even know Joel! Why would you suspect him of anything?*

"Everyone pay attention." Conner clapped his hands. "We have a lot to discuss. I want to go over all of our rules and talk to you about what you will wear on the excavation site. We want everyone to be safe." He opened a large crate and pulled out a yellow hard hat and a bright colored jacket. "You campers will wear these at all times."

"Ooo, a hard hat!" Kate took the bright yellow hat as Megan handed it to her and plopped it on her head. "Ouch. Man, that really is hard."

"Safety equipment is so important here at Stone's Throw because you never know when we'll come across falling rocks," Conner explained. "And staying with the group is critical, too. We don't want to run the risk of anyone getting lost."

"We're also giving you these backpacks to carry your tools in," Megan said. "Any you might have brought from home probably aren't strong enough to hold your accessories and any rocks you might pick up. Remember, many of the rocks will be dirty or muddy."

"Ugh." McKenzie sighed. "So much for staying clean."

"Take a look at your tools now," Conner said.

Kate looked inside her backpack, pulling out a hammer and chisel. "Wow. Cool." She suddenly felt like a real paleontologist.

"Make sure the hammer you've received is the right

weight for you," Conner said. "It can't be too heavy or too light. You'll use it to pound on rocks."

Kate decided hers was just right. Not too big. Not too small. She felt like Goldilocks.

"Next, carefully pull the chisel out of the bag," Conner instructed.

Kate gingerly lifted the chisel from the backpack, her eyes growing wide as she examined it. "Wow."

"Most of your work will be done with this chisel," Conner explained. "You will use it to remove fossils from the surrounding environment. A large chisel, like the one you're holding now, will be used for most of your work. But there's a smaller chisel in the bag to help you handle the more precise work. It will come in handy, too."

"Why?" A younger camper asked.

"A lot of fossils are still buried in stone under many layers of rock. In order to get to them we have to very carefully remove the stone. It's a long and tedious process. I'm warning you now that if you are impatient, these next few days will be very difficult for you."

"I'm pretty patient," Kate whispered. "So I should be okay."

McKenzie shrugged. "I hope I am. I guess we'll find out!"

As Kate looked at her tools, she thought about Mrs. Smith and wondered what she was doing today. How Mrs. Smith would have enjoyed this adventure! Kate could just picture her now, chiseling the stone in search of fossils to put in the museum. How fun!

As she held the chisel in her hand, Kate was reminded of Megan's words. Not only would she dig for fossils this week, she would also dig deep in her Bible to see what she might discover there, too! Of course, she wouldn't need a chisel for that!

Conner continued his teaching, and Kate did her best to pay attention. "There are a couple of other tools in the bag that will come in handy," he said. "You won't always need a hammer or chisel to remove the fossil from its surroundings. You might just need an instrument called a steel point. And of course a brush will come in handy. You'll use it to clean dust and other debris from the fossil."

Kate held up her brush and examined it closely. "Hmm." Things were getting more interesting by the minute.

"There are a handful of other items in your bag," Megan said. "A magnifying lens, of course. And a tiny container of superglue to secure broken fossils. Only use the superglue in case of an emergency. We've also given you foam sheets to wrap your samples in, and elastic bands to secure the foam sheets so that nothing gets broken. You will also find a couple of small boxes to carry tiny samples, as well as plastic bags. Any questions?"

A couple of the kids raised their hands, but Kate was too excited looking at her chisel to ask any questions. She pulled out her tiny digital camera and took a picture.

"I see that Kate has her camera," Megan said.

Kate looked up, embarrassed.

"That's okay, Kate. We encourage you to bring a digital camera so that you can take pictures of the specimens as you find them."

"Whew." Kate smiled. "I thought I was in trouble." She reached into her pocket and pulled out the tiny digital recorder. "Is it okay to use this to record my thoughts when I find something?"

"Of course!" Megan nodded. "Really, the only way you can get in trouble around here is by going off away from the group."

"Or going into the private rooms in the museum," Conner added, suddenly looking a little nervous. "There are a few areas where only quarry staff can go. Just keep an eye out for the No Campers Allowed signs and you'll do just fine."

"Can we make phone calls?" Kate asked.

"Yeah, what if we need to call our parents or something?" McKenzie asked.

"Just make sure you let us know first," Megan said.

Conner nodded. "Yes, and if there's something important enough for your parents to know, we need to know first, especially if you're not feeling well. And speaking of which, I guess it's about time we went over our safety requirements so that you can stay healthy and safe while you're with us."

"I want to check to make sure you're all wearing proper footwear," Megan said. "Boots are best."

She examined everyone's feet. Kate giggled as she looked

down at her hiking boots. They didn't come in very handy back home in Philadelphia, but here, they were perfect!

"Your boots are excellent for this environment, Kate," Megan said, giving them a closer look. "Walking boots protect campers from ankle sprains and keep you from slipping on wet surfaces."

"Wet surfaces?" McKenzie looked up at the sky. "It's not even raining."

"No, but where we're going, some of the terrain will still be covered in morning dew or will be damp from yesterday's light rainfall. We can never be too careful."

"Now, let's talk about eye and hand protection." Megan held up a pair of safety goggles. "Safety glasses must be worn any time you're hammering rocks. Splinters can be very dangerous." She held up a pair of gloves. "These will keep your hands from getting blisters while you're hammering. There's nothing worse than blisters when you've still got work to do. Trust me."

Kate thought about what Sydney had said about wearing sunscreen and drinking lots of water. Thank goodness she had come prepared. Looked like she and McKenzie were going to have to be extra careful this week. Fossil camp just might turn out to be a little dangerous!

She listened closely as Conner and Megan gave them the rest of their instructions. As she did, Kate couldn't help but think about the Camp Club Girls. She wondered what they were doing right now. Was Elizabeth reading that Bible story about Jacob and Esau, trying to get some answers? Had Alex learned anything from her documentary? Would Sydney have any advice about the quarry? Was Bailey pouting because she didn't get to come to fossil camp?

If only she could talk to them right now!

"Kate, would you like to be the first to try out your tools?"

She startled to attention as she heard Conner's voice.

"I. . .I'm sorry. What?"

He gave her a funny look. "Were you daydreaming? I was asking if you would like to be the first one to use your tools to excavate."

"Um, sure." She reached for her chisel and moved to a spot next to him. Then, as he instructed, she began to chip away at the ground. Kate whispered up a prayer, asking the Lord to help her during this very exciting week. What would He unearth? Only time would tell!

Unearthing New Clues

After just a few minutes of digging, Conner and Megan dismissed the campers to the main building for lunch. Kate's tummy grumbled in anticipation. She could hardly wait to eat.

McKenzie looked her way. "What did it feel like, Kate?" she asked. "Using the chisel, I mean."

Kate shrugged. "I didn't really get to dig long enough to find anything, but it was fun."

"It was just a practice run," Megan said, stepping alongside her. "We always choose one camper to demonstrate. You did great! I have a feeling you'll do fine at excavating."

"If I can just pay attention," Kate said, then laughed.

"What do you mean?" Megan looked at her curiously.

"I just mean that my mind wanders," Kate explained. "I'm usually thinking of other things and other people." *Like my teacher. And the Camp Club girls. And Dexter.* For some reason, she couldn't help feeling a little guilty about the fact that she was having so much fun and he was back at Yellowstone without her.

"Well, I don't know about you, but I was thinking about lunch!" Megan laughed. She hollered out to the group. "Follow me to the lunchroom, everyone!"

They walked around the back of the building, past a door that read PRIVATE, and kept going until they came to a door leading to the lunchroom. As they entered, Joel walked beside Kate and McKenzie.

"Did you have fun?" he asked.

"Yes." Kate nodded. "Can I ask you a question, Joel?"

"Sure." He shrugged.

"Can you tell me about the fossils you've found? The valuable ones, I mean. And don't leave out a thing. I have a lot to learn and I have a feeling you could teach me what I need to know."

He nodded. "Sure, but it might be easier to show you. After lunch I'll take you into the museum as we can talk about the fossils I found and actually see them at the same time. Like I said, the most valuable ones are still here. I couldn't take them with me."

McKenzie's eyes widened. "I still can't get over the fact that you're just a camper like us, but you actually have fossils on display here. That's so cool."

He shrugged. "It's really not that big of a deal."

"Not that big of a deal?" Kate stared at him. How could he say that? "Those fossils were buried deep in the earth thousands of years ago! Of course it's a big deal."

When he shrugged again, she thought about how strange

he was acting. Maybe her feelings about him earlier were right. Something about this guy was suspicious. Maybe Joel really wanted Conner's job. Maybe he was really the one who had forged the fossils. But why would he do such a thing? To make someone else look bad, perhaps? None of this made sense. And if he did do it, how would she ever prove it? There was only one way. She had to win his confidence. And then she had to somehow get his fingerprints.

Kate and McKenzie got their trays and walked to the lunch counter to get their food.

"I'm starving!" Kate said. "I can't wait to eat my lunch. Then I'm going back to the cabin and eat some of the cookies my mom packed for me." She gazed at the plate, confused. "What *is* this stuff?" she asked.

"Oh, they always give us fun stuff at mealtime," Joel explained. He pointed to the fish sticks. "They call these Knightia Nuggets. Get it?" She shook her head. "You know. *Knightia,*" Joel repeated.

When she shook her head a second time, he explained. "*Knightia* is an extinct species of fish, found in Wyoming. They're trying to be funny and clever. Today it's fish. Tomorrow they'll probably serve us chicken legs and call them dinosaur bones. It's supposed to get us in the mood to excavate."

"Oooh, I see." Kate smiled.

"Very funny." McKenzie led the way to the table and sat down.

As they ate, the girls from Kate and McKenzie's dorm all gathered around with their food. One of them—what was her name, again? Lauren? Yes, Lauren. She acted as if she had a little crush on Joel. Not that he noticed. He just kept talking about fossils, fossils, and more fossils. Half of the things he talked about Kate could figure out. The rest? Well, some of it just didn't make sense. This guy really knew his stuff!

"Do you feel like you have a lot to learn?" McKenzie whispered in Kate's ear.

She nodded. "Yes, and I don't think a three-day camp is long enough! I never realized how little I knew about all of this. But I'm willing to learn."

"Me, too." McKenzie nodded. "And I can't wait to share what we learn with the other Camp Club Girls."

They enjoyed their lunch and getting to know the others. Kate especially liked Patti, who kept them entertained with stories about her friends at school.

"She reminds me of Bailey," McKenzie whispered.

"I know!" Kate grinned. "I was just thinking the same thing."

Before long, McKenzie told the others about Kate's gadgets. "You should see all of her stuff!" she said. "She has a pen that records text, a miniature camera, a digital recorder, and a wristwatch that sends e-mails."

"No way." Joel looked at her as if he didn't quite believe it.

"It's true." Kate lifted her wrist and showed off the

watch. "I'll send an e-mail right now."

"You're kidding, right?" Lauren asked, looking stunned.

"Nope." She typed a quick e-mail to Elizabeth.

Thanks for your prayers. We made it to the quarry safely.

Then she pushed the tiny SEND button. Joel looked on, still not looking convinced.

A couple of minutes later, the little watch let out a beep and she pushed a button, showing off Elizabeth's e-mail response.

Glad you made it. Talk to you tonight online!

"See!" She held her watch up for Joel to read the note. He shook his head. "Man. That's really something. What else have you got?"

"Oh, bunches of stuff. My dad is a robotics professor. You should see the cool electronics we have at home. Robots galore!"

"No way." Joel stared at her. "Are you serious?"

"Yep. We even have a robotic security system. And a robovac to clean our carpets. His name is Robby."

"Her dad always gives her the neatest things," McKenzie explained.

"Well, sometimes his students invent things and we end

up with the beta versions."

"What's your favorite thing?" he asked.

"Hmm." She thought about it for a minute before answering. "Probably the wristwatch. But I love my mirrored sunglasses, too. They've come in really handy."

"Did you bring them with you?"

"Sure." She shrugged. "I'll wear them to the dig this afternoon if you like."

"That would be cool." He gave her an admiring look and she felt embarrassed. She finished up her meal then quickly changed the subject.

"Do we have time to look in the museum before we head back out to the excavation site?"

"Plenty of time," he said. "They always give us an hour break after lunch, anyway. Would you like to go look at my fossils now?"

"Sure. Why not."

Kate and McKenzie trudged along on his heels as he led the way to the small museum. As they walked inside, Kate noticed an older man with thinning hair carrying some large boxes. He was dressed in dark pants and a Stone's Throw work shirt. Both were wrinkled and dirty. And his hair—what little of it there was—was sticking up on top of his head. In fact, it looked like it hadn't been combed all day.

The sour-faced man grunted as the kids walked by. "You kids watch where you're going and stay out of my way," he mumbled. He began to mutter something under his breath about how kids were always getting under his feet, and Kate took a giant step away from him. She wondered why he was in such a terrible mood.

"Who is that guy?" she whispered as they turned toward the first display.

"Oh, that's Gus," Joel said with a shrug. "He's only been here a couple of years. Gus is the one who packs and ships the fossils. If I were you, I wouldn't bother him. He's a little cranky."

The older man almost dropped one of the boxes.

"See what you did?" he said with a grunt. "You kids made me lose my train of thought. I almost dropped this."

He carried the boxes to the door marked PRIVATE, then put them down on the ground to open it. Seconds later, he disappeared inside.

"What's he cranky about?" McKenzie asked. "We didn't do anything to him."

"I know." Joel shook his head. "I've never been able to figure him out. Trust me. No one has."

"Still, he needs to be nicer to people," Kate said. "There's no excuse for being so mean."

"Sounds like he's got a great job," McKenzie added. "I think it would be fun to prepare the fossils and ship them all over the country. I think it would be a blast. A person with a job like that should be in a good mood!"

"I know." Joel shook his head. "I've never understood why, but he's always moody. I've just learned to stay away from him. And trust me, I've been coming here for years, so I know what I'm talking about. Everyone around here calls him Grumpy Gus."

Kate frowned. "Maybe he's in a bad mood because people stay away from him. I'll be extra nice to him for the next few days and see if I can get him to smile."

"Good luck with that!" Joel laughed. "You won't be the first person to try, and you certainly won't be the last. But I'll bet you can't get him to smile, Kate."

"Oh really!" She took those words as a challenge. Before fossil camp was over, she would get Grumpy Gus to smile, no doubt about it.

As they entered the museum, she looked at the door the older man had walked through. "What's back there?" she asked.

"That's where Gus works," Joel explained. "I've only been back there a couple of times. If you want to know more, ask Conner. He hangs out in there a lot. It's where the fossils are cleaned and prepared for packing."

Kate nodded, but didn't say anything. She couldn't help but try to figure out what lay behind that door with the word PRIVATE on it.

McKenzie cleared her throat and Kate looked her way. "What?" she mouthed.

"I'll tell you later," McKenzie whispered. "Something about that man seemed suspicious. Maybe we can talk about it later this evening when we're alone."

Kate felt a shiver run up her spine and she nodded. Something about Grumpy Gus made her very nervous, too.

They wandered through the museum, looking at all of the displays. "I wish I had more time to explain all of this," Joel said. "But it'll have to be a fast tour."

"That's okay." Kate gave him a warm smile. "We're just happy to be here."

"Thanks." He looked embarrassed. "Remember I talked about the *Knightia* at lunch? This is a sample."

"Wow." Kate stared at it, mesmerized. "It's so. . .perfect."

"Yep." He nodded. "And over here we have several other species of fish. "The *Mioplosus*. The *Diplomystus*."

"Goodness." Kate shook her head. However did he remember those complex words?

After looking at several specimens, they reached the far wall. Joel looked around, his brow wrinkling in confusion. "That's weird," he said.

"What?" McKenzie asked.

"Well, the stingray fossil that I discovered is usually mounted in a box right here, but it's missing. Conner never mentioned anything about taking it down. It's the most valuable fossil of all the ones I've found, so I'm especially proud of it."

"Seems odd that the most valuable one is missing," Kate said, growing more suspicious by the minute. Had Grumpy Gus stolen it? Her imagination almost ran away with her as she thought about the possibilities. Kate pulled out her camera.

"What are you taking a picture of?" McKenzie asked. "There's nothing there to photograph."

"Sure there is." She pointed to the plaque that read HELIOBATIS STINGRAY.

"Why take a picture of that?" Joel asked.

"For research."

He shrugged. "I don't see the point." Shaking his head, he added, "I just wish I knew what happened to my stingray specimen. I dug for hours to get that one. . .and now it's gone."

"Are you worried that someone stole your fossil, Joel?" McKenzie asked.

He shrugged. "I don't know. Could be they've loaned it out to another museum. They do that a lot."

"I know," Kate added. "My teacher is a curator at the science museum in Philadelphia, where I live."

"You're kidding." He gave her an admiring look. "That's impressive."

"I help her sometimes." Kate shrugged. "For fun."

She didn't tell him about the fake fossils they'd discovered. No point in sharing too much information, just in case.

Joel sat on a nearby bench, looking sad. Kate sat down beside him.

"What are you really worried about?" she asked. "You have something on your mind. I can tell."

He sighed. "This is the deal. Every year the quarry offers

a six-week internship to one camper who shows potential. A couple of famous paleontologists are coming to spend the rest of the summer, and I wanted to spend it with them. Can you imagine what an honor that would be?"

"Um, sure." Kate shrugged. Might sound like fun to Joel, but she couldn't imagine spending the whole summer outside digging with chisels in the rock and the dirt.

Joel rose and started to pace back and forth, his brow wrinkled. "That fossil is my best sample. How will they ever know what I'm capable of if it's gone?" He continued to pace.

"Are you worried some other camper will get the internship?" Kate asked.

"Maybe. It's pretty complicated," he explained. "This internship is open to kids all over the world. More than three hundred teenagers have competed for this honor. I really thought I stood a chance. . .until now. Now I'm ready to give up."

"Give up?" McKenzie gave him a curious look. "Over a missing fossil?"

"That stingray fossil is my biggest achievement and now it's gone. There's no proof that I discovered it. It's like someone just walked away with the proof that I'm valuable. That I'm worth anything."

Kate gasped. "Well, of course you're valuable!" She looked at him, stunned, not quite believing he had said that. "You're one of God's kids. We're all valuable in His sight."

Joel shrugged. "You don't get it, Kate. Where I come

from, you have to prove yourself. In my house, you have to get straight As on your report card or make the honor roll at school to get noticed."

"But that doesn't prove you're valuable," McKenzie argued. "Even if you got Bs or struggled in school, you would still be valuable to God."

"Try telling that to my teachers and parents. You girls just don't understand." Joel plopped back down on the bench and sighed.

"I do." Kate sat next to him. "My dad is really, really smart. He's a professor, remember? But he would be the first to tell you that our real value comes from God."

She pointed at the wall. "All of these things are worth a lot of money. I know that. But I also know that you're more valuable to God than all of them put together. And you don't have to prove anything to Him. He loves you, even if you're not always the one who gets the internship or gets straight As."

Joel bit his lip and Kate could tell he was really thinking about what she had said. After a while, he shrugged. "I guess. If you say so." He gave her a funny look then glanced at the clock on the wall. "Oh no! It's five minutes till two. We've got to get back out to the site. This is the best part. The excavation begins right away!"

"Do I have time to get my mirrored sunglasses?" Kate asked.

"Only if you hurry!"

The kids took off running toward the quarry as fast as their legs could go!

CHAPTER
7
★ ★ ★ ★

The Big Dig

Kate ran behind Joel and McKenzie, stopping to get her sunglasses out of the bunkhouse. She arrived at the excavation site huffing and puffing, but right on time.

"Take a look around you," Conner said to the group as he gestured to a large open field. "It's hard to believe, but this area used to be a lake."

Kate paused for a few breaths, then paid close attention.

"Wow. We're standing in the middle of a dried up lake," McKenzie whispered. "Good thing I brought my swimsuit!" She laughed and Kate giggled.

"This region of Wyoming is loaded with fossil specimens," Conner explained. "Thousands of years ago rains would fall and the water would flow down the mountain, forming lakes."

Megan stepped up beside him. "Another theory is that the whole earth was covered in water during the Genesis flood, creating the perfect environment for fish."

"The Genesis flood?" Patti, the little girl with the red hair and freckles, looked confused.

"You know," Kate threw in. "The story of Noah and the ark. It rained for forty days and nights."

"I remember hearing that story in kids' church," Lauren said, tossing her hair. "Can you imagine being on that ark with all of those stinky animals?" She made a face and pinched her nose. "Gross!"

This got all of the girls tickled and before long, everyone was laughing. Well, everyone but Kate. She was still thinking about what Megan had said.

"Regardless," Conner said. "The waters dried. When that happened, millions of fish died in just a short period of time."

"How sad," Kate whispered.

"Because of that, this area is rich in fish fossils," Conner said. "That's good news for us, since that's what we're searching for today." He gestured to his right. "Layers of mud covered up the dead fish of course, but then volcanic activity occurred."

"Volcanoes?" McKenzie looked very, very nervous. Her eyes grew big.

"That happened a long time ago," Conner explained. "Not any more."

"Whew." McKenzie looked relieved.

"Anyway, the volcanic activity exposed the fish fossils. And thousands upon thousands of them are still here, waiting to be discovered. . .by you!"

"Wow." Kate could hardly believe it. Would she really find a fossil? If so, would she get to keep it, or would they put it in a box and hang it on a wall in the museum? Suddenly she could hardly wait to get started.

"I know you kids are anxious," Conner said. "But there are a few things we need to cover before we actually start digging." He held up something small. Kate took a couple of steps toward him to see what it was.

"This is a *Mioplosus* specimen. They are very common in this region. I'm going to explain how it became a fossil, so pay close attention."

Kate drew near, more excited than ever.

"There are five phases to fossilization," Conner explained. "You might need your notepads for this one. You'll want to remember all of this for later on."

Kate leaned over to Megan and whispered, "Can I use my digital recorder?"

"Of course," Megan nodded. "He'll cover a lot of material, so taking notes would be tough anyway."

Kate reached inside her backpack and came out with the tiny black digital recorder and turned it on.

Conner held up the fossil and explained. "The first phase of fossilization is death," he said. "Let's say, for example, that a fish dies, then drifts to the bottom of the lake. After scavengers get a hold of it, the skeleton is the only thing that remains."

"Gross," McKenzie whispered. "Doesn't sound very appetizing."

"Oh, but that's the most important part," Joel said softly.

"Sometimes bad things have to happen in order for good things to come out of them."

"Hmm." Kate thought about his words. Sometimes life was like that. Bad things happened. . .then good things came out of the bad.

"After death comes the deposition stage," Conner explained. "During this phase, the sand and silt cover up the shell over a period of time, building several layers."

"Those layers protect the shell from damage," Kate whispered. "I read all about it online."

"Yeah, I saw a video in my science class about this," McKenzie whispered back. "After hundreds of years, the shell is way below the surface. No one even knows it's there."

"Right." Kate nodded. "Sometimes for thousands of years. Can you imagine?"

McKenzie shook her head.

Kate was lost in her thoughts when Conner started talking once again.

"After the deposition comes the third phase," he explained. "We call this permineralisation."

"Per-mineralisation?" Little Patti shook her head. "I hope I don't have to spell that word later. I'll never get it right."

Megan offered a smile. "Break the word down into parts. Per-mineral-is-a-tion. It just means the shell goes through a bunch of changes over time. Before long, the original shell becomes hard, like a rock."

"Why didn't he just say that?" Patti mumbled.

Conner went on to talk about that process, but Kate was distracted, watching Joel, who was scribbling notes in his notebook. He really was taking this seriously. She felt bad for him, knowing his fossils were missing. On the other hand, maybe they really had just been loaned to another museum. She hoped so, anyway.

Conner continued explaining how fossils were made, and Kate tried to pay attention, even though some of what he said didn't make much sense.

"The fourth phase is erosion," Conner said. "Wind, ice, sun, and rain begin to take their toll on the fossil, changing it."

"Everything changes over time," Joel whispered, still scribbling in his notebook.

Kate looked over at McKenzie, who had changed so much over the past year, and nodded. "Yep. It's true," she whispered.

Conner continued to talk. "Finally, the last phase. Exposure. Exposure comes when a paleontologist locates the fossil. It is removed from the ground and is cleaned up."

"That's what I do," Joel said, squaring his shoulders. "Finding them is the best part!"

Kate tried to pay attention, but every time she thought about someone cleaning the fossils, she remembered Grumpy Gus. What did he do behind closed doors besides cleaning and packing fossils? Did he have a mold and several bags of brown sugar, perhaps? Did he take the real fossil plates and sell them illegally and pocket the money?

Was he the one who had stolen Joel's fossils? Was he the one responsible for what happened to poor Mrs. Smith?

Kate's imagination began to work overtime as she thought about it.

"After a fossil is exposed, we look at it under a magnifying lens," Megan said. "Examine every square inch of it."

"That's the fun part," Joel whispered. "Seeing everything close up. Have you ever looked at a fossil through a magnifying lens? It's really cool."

"Yes, actually, I. . ." she started to tell him about that day at the museum with her teacher, but stopped. No, she couldn't give away too much information just yet. After all, she still wasn't sure who she could trust. Joel might look like a good guy, but he could be faking it. She needed to be on the lookout for fakes. . .no doubt about that.

"How big are fossils, anyway?" McKenzie asked.

"Oh, they come in all shapes and sizes," Conner explained. "Some are so tiny you can only see them with a magnifying lens, and some are huge. Some of the bigger ones include bones belonging to dinosaurs."

"Wow." The girl's eyes grew wide at this news. "Really?" Conner nodded.

Kate raised her hand. "Excuse me, but can I ask a question?"

"Sure," Conner said.

"What happens to the fossils when they leave the quarry? Do you sell them?"

Conner appeared to be thinking about his answer. "As

we've discussed, many of the fossils are quite valuable. Those stay here at the museum but are often loaned to other museums around the country. People all over the country enjoy looking at Stone's Throw fossils. They're quite popular."

When they're real, Kate thought.

"You'd be very surprised at just how valuable some of these fossils are," he added. "And how rare."

"So valuable and rare that someone wants to steal them and keep the money for themselves!" McKenzie whispered.

Kate nodded, then looked at Joel. She couldn't stop thinking about the missing stingray. Was Joel the victim? Or was he somehow involved in all of this? Only time would tell.

"Okay, kids!" Megan clapped her hands to get their attention. "It's time to get suited up! We're going to start our first dig. So grab those hard hats! Put on those safety goggles! Let's get digging!"

Kate scrambled into her bright orange jacket, put on her yellow hard hat, and grabbed her goggles. After securing them, she reached for her backpack and pulled out the larger chisel.

"I'm ready!" she said with a giggle.

The next hour was spent digging. At first, it seemed easy. But after a while, Kate's arms got really tired. "I don't think I could be a paleontologist," she whispered to McKenzie. "My arms aren't strong enough!"

"What would Elizabeth say to that?" McKenzie whispered back.

"I know, I know." Kate laughed. "She would say, 'I can do all things through Christ who strengthens me.'"

"And she's right," McKenzie said. "Besides. . ." She flexed the muscles in her upper arm. "We're getting stronger every day."

"Getting stronger every day. I like that." Kate nodded, and then slowly began to dig again.

Before long, one of the girls hollered, and Kate turned around, curious.

"I found one!" Lauren said with a joyous look. "I really, really found one! Look everyone!"

They all drew near and examined the fossil.

"It's broken, but it's still really cool." She held it out for Conner to examine.

"Yes, that's a *Knightia*," he said. "They are very common here in Wyoming. Nicely done, Lauren. You're the first to unearth a fossil, so you'll get the privilege of leading one of the teams in the treasure hunt tomorrow morning."

"Aw man." Kate shrugged. "Wish I'd been the first."

"What would Elizabeth say?" McKenzie asked her again.

Kate grinned. "She would quote the scripture 'But many who are first will be last, and the last first.'"

"Exactly." McKenzie nodded. "So let's remember that. And just because we're not the first to discover a fossil doesn't mean we won't figure out who forged the ones at your teacher's museum. We're here for a reason, Kate, and I truly believe the Lord will do something very exciting!"

Kate was starting to nod when something—or rather, someone—in the distance caught her eye. "Look, McKenzie!" She pointed as an older man disappeared behind the trees to their left. "Was that Grumpy Gus?"

"No idea. I didn't get a good look."

Kate reached into her bag and came up with her teensy-tiny binoculars. She pulled off her safety glasses and peered into the binoculars, trying to see into the forest. Yes, sure enough, a man was running, hiding from tree to tree. She couldn't tell for sure, but it looked like Gus. He was wearing the same color shirt, anyway.

"Something is very suspicious here, McKenzie," she whispered. "Very suspicious, indeed!"

Camp Club Girls to the Rescue!

Later that evening, the campers headed into the dining hall. Something smelled really good!

"What's for dinner?" Kate asked as they sat down at the table.

"Just as I predicted." Joel held up a chicken leg. "Dinosaur bones. *Tyrannosaurus rex*!"

McKenzie shook her head as she picked up the piece of chicken. "Doesn't look like any *Tyrannosaurus rex* I've ever seen!"

"Exactly." Joel slapped himself in the head and Kate laughed.

"Well, the cook has a great sense of humor, anyway!" she said.

She got into the line to get her food but something caught her eye. "McKenzie!" She elbowed her friend.

"Ouch!" McKenzie rubbed her side. "What is it, Kate?"

"Look." She pointed at Gus, who carried a large bag of brown sugar.

"Ooo." McKenzie nodded. "And look, Kate. . .he's

headed away from the kitchen, not toward it. Isn't that strange?"

"Very."

"What are you girls talking about?" Lauren stepped into line behind them and started chatting about the fossil she had found. Before long, as they talked, Kate almost forgot about Gus. Almost.

When she got back to the table with her food, Kate joined a fun conversation with Joel and the other campers, laughing and talking about their adventures at the camp. Someone in the room started clapping, so she looked up, curious.

"We have a wonderful treat for you kids tonight," Megan said, getting everyone's attention. "I want to introduce someone very special to me."

An older man entered the room. He had soft white hair and wore blue jeans and a button-up cowboy shirt. His long white moustache and beard reminded Kate of someone from an old movie. And his leathery, tanned skin surely proved that he spent a lot of time in the sun.

"This is my father, Gerald Jenkins," Megan said proudly. "He is the owner of Stone's Throw Quarry."

"Wow." So this was Megan's dad.

Mr. Jenkins joined the campers, answering many of their questions. Kate finally worked up the courage to ask her question, but waited until the others were distracted, so they wouldn't hear her.

"Mr. Jenkins?" She spoke softly and he looked her way. "My name is Kate Oliver. I live in Philadelphia and my teacher works for the Museum of Natural Science as a curator."

"Ah." He nodded. "I can guess what you're about to ask."

Kate bit her lip, trying to decide how much to share. Finally she could take it no longer and blurted out her question. "Do you know about the fake fossils that my teacher and I found? If so, do you have any idea who forged them?"

"Yes, I know all about it," he said, keeping his voice low. "Your teacher called last week. I contacted the police and they've been out to take a report. But I can't figure out who is doing this to us. We've been sabotaged, for sure."

"You haven't seen anyone with brown sugar? Or anyone acting strangely?" *Like Grumpy Gus, for instance?*

"Not on the property. And I've looked, trust me." He shook his head. "I'm here all day every day and haven't seen anything suspicious."

She thought about telling Mr. Jenkins that she and McKenzie had just seen Gus carrying a large bag of brown sugar, but didn't. Not yet, anyway. She had to be sure she could trust him first.

He shook his head and his eyes grew misty. "I feel terrible about what happened," Mr. Jenkins said. "But I feel even worse when I think about the fact that someone stole the original fossil plates from us. They're worth a lot of money."

"What would a person do with stolen fossils, anyway?" Kate asked.

"Oh, all sorts of things. They're valued all over the world, so maybe they sold them to an underground ring of fossil thieves."

"Ooo, sounds scary."

"Another theory is that they are holding them for ransom. Maybe to try to bribe me in some way."

"Why would someone do that?" Kate asked.

He shrugged. "I don't know. I can only tell you that I've been praying about this all week, ever since I got the call from your teacher." He smiled at Kate. "We'll figure out who did this. . .with the Lord's help. Those fossils will return home to Stone's Throw, and I'll send them to your teacher for the exhibit. You just wait and see."

"I hope you're right." She paused a moment, then looked into his kind eyes. "Can I ask you one more question?"

"Sure."

"Joel is a great camper and he knows so much."

"Oh yes, he's one of the best," Mr. Jenkins agreed.

Kate bit her lip as she tried to decide how much to say next. "He's worried he won't get the internship because his stingray fossil is gone."

"What?" Mr. Jenkins looked stunned. "The stingray is missing, too?"

Kate nodded. "We don't know that it's officially missing. I was hoping you loaned it to another museum."

"No." He shook his head. "We often loan out fossils, as you know, but everything is written on a schedule. I don't remember anything about the stingray being loaned out. Very strange."

"Well if you go into the museum, you'll see that it's missing," Kate said.

"I'll do that right now," he said. He nodded. "Thank you for the information, Kate."

"You're welcome, sir. Thanks for letting us come to your great quarry!"

After she finished eating, Kate headed back to the cabin with McKenzie at her side.

"So what did Mr. Jenkins say?" McKenzie asked.

"He knows all about the fake fossils," she said. "And he says he's praying about it." She paused a moment. "He didn't seem to know anything about the missing stingray though."

"Odd, isn't it?" McKenzie observed. "People who work right here don't seem to notice much, do they?"

"Wow." Kate paused to think about that. "You might be on to something there, McKenzie. We saw Grumpy Gus walking across the dining hall with a bag of brown sugar, and yet Mr. Jenkins says he's been watching, but hasn't seen anything suspicious. What's up with that?"

"Right." McKenzie paused. "What if Mr. Jenkins is only pretending to be concerned? What if he's really the one who did all of this?"

"Why would he sabotage his own quarry?" Kate asked.

"Doesn't make any sense."

"Sure it does." McKenzie nodded. "It's a great scam. He makes money by selling the real fossils to the bad guys and makes money by selling the fakes to legitimate businesses. That's a lot of money!"

"I don't know, McKenzie." Kate shook her head as they entered the cabin, then paused to give her a serious look. "It would break Megan's heart to find out that her dad was doing something illegal."

"True." McKenzie sighed.

Kate walked over to her bunk and sat down, whispering so the other girls wouldn't hear. "I'm not really accusing Mr. Jenkins. I'm just thinking out loud. Trying to figure out who did this."

"I know. And the suspects are piling up." McKenzie reached for a rubber band and pulled her hair up into a ponytail. "But that's why we're meeting with the other Camp Club Girls tonight in the chat room, right?" She paused. "I can't wait to tell them what we found out today."

"Before we talk to them, can I ask you a question?" Kate asked.

"Sure."

"Remember you said there was something suspicious about Gus? What did you mean?"

"Oh. . ." McKenzie's brow wrinkled. "I just noticed his clothes were really wrinkled, like maybe he slept in them or something."

"I noticed that, too!" Kate said. "It was a little strange, wasn't it?"

"Yes. What kind of a person is so busy that he can't even change into pajamas to sleep?" McKenzie said. "It makes me think he's up to something in the middle of the night."

"Ooo, I see." Kate nodded.

"Maybe." McKenzie nodded. "The wrinkles in his clothes make me wonder."

"Well, we can ask the other girls their opinion."

"What other girls?" Patti asked, plopping on Kate's bed. "What are you girls whispering about, anyway?"

"Yes, what's up with you two?" Lauren asked, joining them. "You've been acting mighty suspicious!"

"Oh, I, um. . ." Kate paused and looked at McKenzie. She didn't know how much she should share with these girls. After all, she barely knew them!

"Kate and I are on a secret adventure," McKenzie said. "We'll tell you all about it tomorrow or the next day."

"But we leave day after tomorrow," Patti argued. "I don't want to wait till then to find out your secret! Tell me now."

Kate shook her head. "What's the point in calling it a secret if I tell it? But I will give you a clue. We're trying to solve a mystery. Trying to figure something out."

"Hmm. A mystery." Patti sighed. "How can I help you if I don't know what it is?"

Kate shrugged. Thankfully, her phone rang at that very moment, interrupting their conversation. She was surprised to hear Alexis's voice on the other end of the line.

"Kate, I know we're meeting with the others online in a few minutes, but I wanted to talk to you first. This is important."

"Sure." Kate rose from the bunk and went outside the cabin so that she could speak to Alexis privately. "What's up?"

"I've been doing some research on the staff at Stone's Throw," Alexis said. "I got the idea after watching that Paleo-World documentary again."

"What did you find out?"

"All of their pictures are on the Web site, along with their names. There's a fellow name Gerald Jenkins who owns the place."

"That's Megan's father," Kate said. "Megan is our counselor."

"Right. Megan Jenkins. She was practically raised at the quarry. And there's a guy named Conner who has all sorts of degrees. He's a paleontologist."

"He's really young," Kate said. "Probably just twenty-five or so."

"From what I can gather, he's really smart. He started as an intern at the quarry a long time ago, and now he's back, working as a counselor."

"Right," Kate said. "Anything else?"

"Yes." Alexis's voice grew more serious. "There's a guy named Gus who seemed a little suspicious to me."

Kate's heart began to thump. "He seems odd to us, too!" she said. "What did you find out about him?"

"Well, I don't want to scare you, but he used to work for another quarry and he got fired. I read about it online. There was a big write-up in the paper a couple of years back. I had to dig deep to find it."

"Dig deep?" Kate couldn't help but smile as Alexis used the words she'd been hearing so much. "Do you know why he was fired?"

"Something to do with some fossils that were accidentally destroyed. Just promise me you'll be careful around him, okay? I would feel terrible if something happened to you girls."

"I'm sure we'll be fine," Kate said. "But we'll be extra careful, just in case. And Alex. . .thank you for calling and telling me that."

"You're welcome. I'll keep researching online to see if I can find out anything else about him."

"Thanks. See you online in a few minutes," Kate said. As she clicked the END button on her phone, Megan walked by.

"Well hello, Kate. Everything okay?"

"Y—yes." She forced a smile. She didn't want Megan to know she suspected anyone just yet. "I was talking to my friend Alex."

"Friends are an important part of our lives, aren't they?" Megan smiled. "God has blessed me with such great friends over the years."

She began to talk about her best friend—someone named Julia—and Kate sighed in relief. At least Megan hadn't asked about the case!

A few minutes later, Kate and McKenzie sat on Kate's bed with the laptop open.

"I sure hope the wireless Internet signal is strong," Kate mumbled. "The other girls are probably already in the chat room waiting on us."

Thankfully, she signed on with no problem at all. Less than a minute later, she was in the chat room and could see that all of the others were already there, just as she predicted. Kate typed while McKenzie looked on.

Bailey: *Hi, K8!*
Elizabeth: *Having a fossil-tastic adventure?*
Kate: *Yes. We've learned a lot already!*
Sydney: *About the case, I hope. I've been working hard on this end!*
Kate: *Good. Before we get started, I wanted to ask a favor. I'm going to upload a picture that I took today. I need someone to spend a little time looking up this fossil online to see if you can locate it. It's missing from the quarry's museum.*

She quickly uploaded the picture of the tiny stingray sign.

Bailey: *What is that, Kate?*
Elizabeth: *Yes, I've never seen anything like that.*

Kate: *It's a very valuable fossil that one of the campers—a guy named Joel—unearthed last summer. For the past year it's been on display in the museum. But today, when he went to show it to me, he noticed it was missing. We don't know if someone took it down for a reason or if it's been stolen.*

Alexis: *Why not just ask someone?*

Kate: *I don't want to raise any red flags. But it makes me curious, especially in light of the forged fossils. Maybe this is a bigger case than we thought! I'm hoping one of you can figure out what happened to it. Maybe if we can track down that fossil, we'll find our answer.*

Sydney: *Leave it to me. I'll find that missing stingray if I have to swim upstream to do it!*

McKenzie laughed at that one.

Elizabeth: *I've been reading the story of Jacob and Esau a lot over the past week or so. And I've prayed and prayed, asking the Lord to show me how it fits with this case.*

Kate: *What has He shown you?*

Elizabeth: *Only that we have to be careful not to be fooled by people who are pretending to be something they're not. Sometimes people put on a big smile and act nice, but on the inside they're really not.*

A shiver ran down Kate's spine. She thought at once of Grumpy Gus. Maybe Elizabeth was right. Maybe he was on the run from the law. Maybe he was just pretending to be a quarry worker.

On the other hand, what about Mr. Jenkins? Sometimes the most honest-looking person turned out to be the real bad guy.

And then there was Joel! Hadn't she already suspected him?

Kate: *I'm so confused. The list of suspects is growing by the minute. I sure hope we can figure this out. Only two more days of camp left! I brought my finger-printing kit, so I hope to lift some prints soon.*

Alexis: *My uncle works in a fingerprinting lab. Maybe he would help.*

Kate: *Great idea!*

Sydney: *We'll figure this out! We're the Camp Club Girls, after all!*

Elizabeth: *And we have the Lord on our side. There's power when people agree in prayer!*

"She's right," McKenzie told Kate. "Six of us are all agreeing and praying!"

"True." Kate smiled, suddenly feeling better. She glanced at the screen, noticing Bailey's next comment:

Bailey: *I wish I could be there with you. How is Biscuit?*
Kate: *He's with my parents. He's not here.*
Bailey: *Not there? How do you expect to solve a mystery without him?*

"She's right, you know," McKenzie said, reading over her shoulder. "Things would be easier with Biscuit here."

Kate sighed. "Megan was really nice to say I could use my gadgets. I don't think she would be as nice if I asked to bring my dog to fossil camp!"

"You never know." McKenzie shrugged. "Maybe you could ask your dad to bring him when he picks us up. Might be fun. Ask Megan first, though."

"I'll do that." Kate turned her attention back to the screen, smiling as she read Elizabeth's last line.

Elizabeth: *I have to sign off now, but I will be praying. Remember that Jacob and Esau story. Don't let anyone fool you into thinking they're something—or someone— they're not. Okay?*

All of the girls said their good-byes and before long the chat room was empty. Kate turned to McKenzie and sighed. "Looks like we've got to be extra careful, now that the suspects are piling up."

"Suspects?" Patti's voice rang out. "What do you mean?" She sat on the edge of Kate's bed.

"Yes," Lauren said, joining them. "Sounds like this secret thing you're working on is getting exciting. Are you sure you can't tell us something about it?"

Kate shook her head. "I promise we'll tell you later. Right now I need to pray about all of this."

"Did I hear someone say something about praying?" Megan's voice rang out as she entered the room, her hair still wet from the shower.

"Yes." Kate nodded. "I've got a lot on my mind."

"Well prayer is the answer." Megan winked. Drawing near to Kate, she whispered, "Remember what I told you earlier today. Spend some time digging in your Bible while you're here. Do a little excavation in the scriptures. I think God will shine some light on your situation. . .whatever it is."

Kate nodded. "Okay. I'll do it." She smiled at her counselor, and then thought about all of the questions rolling around in her mind. Who forged the fossils? Why was Gus so grumpy? Was Joel somehow involved in all of this? And what about Mr. Jenkins? Was he just pretending not to know who replaced the real fossils with fakes?

Kate padded off to the showers, her mind reeling in several directions at once. Tonight she had more questions than answers. Hopefully, tomorrow she would have more answers than questions.

Sugar, Sugar

Early the next morning—long before the sun came up—a loud clanging woke Kate.

"What is that?" she grumbled, sitting up in the bed.

"It's the quarry bell," Megan said, stretching. "It goes off every morning at five thirty."

"F–five thirty?" McKenzie bounded up from her slumber. "A–are you kidding me?"

"Nope." Megan laughed. "I'm used to it."

"Well I'm not." Kate yawned.

"Why are we up at five thirty?" Lauren asked from a bed on the other side of the room.

Megan yawned. "It's better to work early in the morning before it gets too hot. Besides, we have a busy day planned for you kids. The sooner we get going, the more we'll accomplish."

"Ugh." Kate rolled over in the bed and pulled the covers up over her head, wishing she could catch a few more Zs. Unfortunately, the bell started clanging again. She pushed the covers back and got out of bed, heading into the bathroom to change into her clothes.

"What time is breakfast?" she heard McKenzie asking Megan.

"Six o'clock. And the excavation begins at seven," Megan explained. "But I think that still leaves you girls plenty of time to read your Bibles and pray, if you'd like to do that before breakfast."

Kate yawned as she thought about the busy day ahead. She was tempted to skip her Bible reading and just go straight to breakfast, but decided against it. Maybe God had something He wanted to show her in the Bible. She reached for her laptop and signed on to the Internet, going at once to her favorite online Bible site.

"Where is the story of Jacob and Esau again?" she whispered to McKenzie.

"I think it's in Genesis. . .right?" McKenzie didn't look convinced.

"Maybe." Kate began to type in the words Jacob and Esau until the scripture came up. "It's Genesis, chapter 25," she said. Skimming over it was the easy part. Trying to figure out what a story about two brothers had to do with this case was quite another! She read the story more carefully the second time, really thinking about it as she did.

"So Jacob wanted something that rightfully belonged to his brother Esau. He wanted his birthright. . .right?"

"I think that's it," McKenzie said.

"To get it, Jacob dressed up in a hairy costume and

pretended to be Esau so his father would give him the blessing that really belonged to his brother." She stopped reading and thought. "Sometimes people really *do* pretend to be one thing when they're really another," she whispered. "People aren't always who we think they are."

"Are you thinking of someone in particular?" McKenzie whispered.

"Maybe." She shook her head. Who did she suspect the most, after all? Gus? Mr. Jenkins? Joel? It would be hard to say at this point.

She wrapped up her Bible study and walked to the dining hall with the others. Once inside, Kate noticed Gus standing near the kitchen door. She nudged McKenzie.

"Look. There he is again."

"He still looks grumpy," McKenzie said. "I think we need to stay away from him."

"I'm not so sure." Kate paused. "Hey, I have an idea." She looked down at her lunch tray and saw the two doughnuts. "I'm going to try an experiment. Watch and see. I'll make him smile."

McKenzie shook her head. "I don't think so, Kate."

"It never hurts to try." Kate walked over to him, and he looked up from his work.

"What do you need, kid?" he asked.

"Oh, nothing. I just wanted to give you something." She reached out showed him the doughnut. He looked at her with a stunned expression.

"What's that for?"

Kate shrugged. "Just because. I thought you might like it."

"Well I don't. I'm diabetic. Can't eat sugar. What are you trying to do? Kill me? Did some of those kids tell you to do that?"

She put the doughnut back on her tray, suddenly nervous. "No. No one said a word about it. And I'm sorry. I didn't know you were diabetic. I was just trying to be nice."

"Well be nice to someone else. I have work to do."

"But. . ." She watched as he disappeared through the door with the No Campers Allowed sign above it. As he disappeared from sight, a creepy feeling came over her. She still wondered what he did back in that room. Sure, he probably shipped fossils. But what else?

"That didn't go very well, did it?" McKenzie asked, drawing near.

"No." Kate shook her head. "He's diabetic. Who knew?"

"Oh wow. And you offered him sugar, of all things."

"Yes, he thought I did it on purpose. Can you believe that?"

"Well maybe other people have been mean to him," McKenzie said. "You never know."

"Maybe." Kate sighed. "But McKenzie. If he's diabetic, why was he carrying around a jumbo-sized bag of brown sugar yesterday? Answer that."

McKenzie shrugged. "I have no idea, but you're right. It doesn't make sense! I will say this though. If he's claiming to be a diabetic, that's the perfect cover."

"What do you mean?" Kate asked.

"I mean, no one would ever suspect a diabetic of using sugar to forge anything. See?"

"Ooo yeah. Good point." Kate nodded. "Gus will be a tough nut to crack. But I feel like we need to know more about him."

"It's getting more and more obvious that he is behind this, don't you think?" McKenzie asked.

Kate shrugged. "Maybe. Only time will tell. One thing is for sure. He has access. He's in that room all alone."

"True."

A familiar voice interrupted their conversation. Conner walked by carrying a large bag. "Hey, kids." He flashed a warm smile. "What did you think of the breakfast?"

"Good." Kate nodded. "I really liked the doughnuts."

"Doughnuts?" He held one up. "Girls, these aren't doughnuts. They're life preservers!" Conner doubled over in laughter and before long they all joined him.

"He's really funny," Kate whispered.

"Yeah," McKenzie nodded. "And he's a great counselor, too. I heard some of the guys talking about him yesterday. They really like him a lot."

"Just like we like Megan."

Conner shifted his bag to his other arm. "We're going to have a great morning, but I need to drop off these samples first. See you soon." He walked through the door into the private area.

"Maybe Conner will catch Grumpy Gus in the act," Kate whispered.

"Maybe." McKenzie shrugged.

Kate yawned as Megan passed by.

"Sleepy, Kate?" her counselor asked.

"Sort of."

"Didn't you sleep well?"

"Not really." She shook her head.

"Miss your family?" Megan asked.

"Sort of, but I have something else on my mind. It's hard to sleep when your thoughts are tumbling around in your head."

"Anything I can do to help?" Megan asked.

Kate shook her head, knowing better than to say too much.

Megan said, "The second day at fossil camp is always the best. We're going to have a treasure hunt."

"Treasure hunt?" McKenzie looked confused.

"Yes, we'll divide the campers into two teams—boys and girls. I'll lead the girls' team and Conner will lead the boys'. We'll give you kids a list of fossils—three different kinds—and the first team to find all three wins."

She began to talk about the treasure hunt so much that Kate found it hard to focus. She kept yawning. Hopefully she would wake up before heading out to excavate. She needed to pay close attention today. Surely an adventure lay ahead!

The Treasure Hunt

As the campers gathered at the excavation site, Conner turned to them with a smile.

"I have some news for you," he said. "Most of you know Joel." He gestured to Joel, whose cheeks turned red.

"Because of Joel's skill in locating valuable fossils, he's our resident 'rock' star." Conner slapped his knee and laughed. "Get it? Rock star?"

Kate laughed. So did McKenzie. But not Megan. She rolled her eyes and whispered, "Don't let Conner distract you. He's just trying to get you girls worked up to think the boys are better than you are. He pulls something like this at every camp."

Kate giggled. "I won't let him get to me, I promise."

Conner rubbed his hands together in excitement. "What we're about to do is my favorite thing at fossil camp. We're going to have a treasure hunt."

"Let's divide into teams," Megan instructed. "Girls, come and get in line behind me, and boys, you line up behind Conner."

Everyone quickly got into place.

"I can tell you're excited," Conner said. "But try to stay calm, cool, and collected. That's the best way to win this challenge." He reached for his clipboard and pulled off two pieces of paper. "Each team has a list of three items. Three different kinds of fossils—*Mioplosus*, *Phareodus*, and *Knightia*. You will see the pictures here." He turned the paper to face them. "The first team to return here to this spot with all three fossils will win."

"What do we win?" McKenzie asked.

Conner's face lit with excitement. "The winning team gets to go into the prep room to watch me clean and prepare the fossils. Then we'll show you the process of packaging and shipping them all over the world."

He began to talk about all of the work that went on in the quarry's prep lab, how the lab tech worked carefully to remove rock from ancient fossils, then prepare them for handling. The whole thing sounded really complicated. . . and exciting!

Kate's heart began to race. How wonderful it would be to get in that room! She would take her fingerprint tape and look for prints. Maybe they would match the ones on the fossils back home. Then perhaps Alexis's uncle could help the girls figure out whose prints they were!

"Conner does most of his work in that room," Megan said. "He's one of the best in the nation. He gets the fossils stabilized, cleaned, and prepared. Then Gus—I believe some of you met him—gets the fossils packaged to send out."

"We've got to get in that room!" McKenzie whispered. "So let's win the treasure hunt."

Kate nodded.

"It's really an amazing honor," Joel explained. "I've only been in there a couple of times over the years. The prep lab is usually off-limits to campers and quarry guests. But it's by far the coolest place here." He began to explain the process of cleaning the fossils, but Kate couldn't keep up with him, he was talking so fast.

"All we have to do is win the treasure hunt," Kate said. "And then I'll get to see it for myself."

"Not possible!" He laughed. "Sorry, girls, but this is my specialty. I'll find all three specimens before you find even one!"

"Campers, let's get suited up," Megan announced as she handed out hard hats, vests, and jackets. Then she gave the campers their backpacks, which were loaded down with tools.

"I feel like I gain ten pounds when I put this on," Patti complained as she struggled to get the backpack in place.

"Just think of how strong your muscles are getting," Megan said with a wink.

Kate couldn't help but think of Dexter. He would have loved this part. Maybe she could do more than win the treasure hunt today. Maybe she would locate a fossil that she could give him. . .something really special. That would make him feel better about not being there. And maybe—she grew more excited as she thought about it—maybe she and McKenzie would find enough fossils for each of the Camp Club Girls, too! Wouldn't Bailey and the others love that!

"Everybody ready?" Conner hollered.

When the campers cheered, Conner lifted his hand and hollered, "On your mark, get set. . ." As he shouted "go!" he dropped his hand. The girls took off running toward the dry lake bed and the boys headed off to the field to their right.

When they arrived, Kate and the others paused to catch their breath. She didn't want to start out feeling so winded, especially when she hadn't had much sleep.

"I'm going to dig for a *Mioplosus*," Lauren said. "My brother found one of those last year when he came to camp."

"I would suggest starting with the *Knightia*," Megan said. "The quarry is filled with them."

Kate watched out of the corner of her eye as Joel went to work with his large chisel. "Man, he's fast," she whispered to McKenzie. "He really knows what he's doing."

"You won't find any fossils if you spend all of your time worrying about how much better he is than us," McKenzie whispered back.

"I know you're in a hurry to get started," Megan said, "but I always like to say a few words before the hunt begins. If you listen to my advice, you'll be more likely to find fossils quickly."

Kate paid close attention.

"Okay, girls, this is what you do." Megan's voice grew serious. "Notice that this whole area is filled with flat slabs of rock. It was formed a long time ago on the bed of the lake."

"Bed of the lake," Kate whispered. Sounded funny.

"You heard Conner explain yesterday how fossils are made. Can you remind me how the fossils got here, in the dry lake bed?"

Kate raised her hand. "Yes. When a fish died, it would sink to the bottom of the lake, then get covered with mud, just like Conner talked about yesterday."

"That's right," Megan said. "And over a long period of time, the lake dried up and the mud turned to stone. So buried deep within those slabs of stone are priceless treasures. In order to find them, you have to pick up the rock and split it. You might be surprised at what you find inside."

Kate paused to think about how life was sometimes like that. Sometimes you really thought you knew someone. . . knew them really well. Then, after a little digging, you learned something else entirely new about them. For example, after a little digging, she had learned that McKenzie snored. Only a little, but still it was a snore. And hadn't she learned a lot about each of the Camp Club Girls since they started solving mysteries together?

"This is one of the things I love most about leading excavations," Megan said. "Sometimes I look around at all of the reminders of life that came before us, thousands of years ago. It's pretty amazing, really, when you think about it. We can hold the past in our hands." She looked at the group, her eyes getting a little misty. "Then I look at all of you campers and I realize that I'm looking at our future. So the past and future come together every year when we lead these excavations. That means so much to me."

"Oh wow." Kate swallowed hard. How interesting, to think that she was part of a project that represented the future. Carrying on a project with fossils formed thousands of years ago.

"When I look at all of you, I also realize that each of you is a treasure, far more valuable than anything we could ever find in the stones here. You are created in God's image. His imprint is in your heart."

Kate smiled as she thought of that. Her mom often told her how much she was loved. Still, it felt good to have someone she barely knew tell her just how precious she was. Megan's words made her day!

"Now go dig up some fossils," Megan said. "But while you do, remember how valuable you are. How priceless."

Kate headed off with her chisel in hand. She found a spot and began to dig. All around her the other girls were laughing and talking, but she didn't join in. Who had time to chat with so much at stake? She had to find those fossils to win the prize! Then she and McKenzie could figure out who was forging the fossils and help Mrs. Smith keep her job.

The morning passed with the girls working extra hard. Kate let out a holler as she located a *Knightia* and the girls all cheered. However, off in the distance they heard the boys cheering, too.

"Sounds like we're tied!" Megan said. "So keep at it, girls. You can do this."

About a half hour later Lauren located a *Mioplosus*. She beamed with joy as she held it up for all to see. "I knew it!" she said. "I knew I would find one!"

"You did a great job!" Megan said, examining the fossil. "I'm so proud of you. Now if we can just find the *Phareodus*. Then you girls will win the treasure hunt and you can tour the prep lab!"

From the other side of the dry lake bed, Kate heard Joel's voice ring out. "I found it!" he shouted. "I found the *Phareodus*!"

"We have all three!" another one of the boys hollered. "The boys win!"

They began to cheer. Kate let go of her chisel, watching it drop to the ground. "They. . .they beat us?"

McKenzie sighed. "Looks like it."

"But how will we ever get into that back room now?" Kate whispered. "This whole trip to Wyoming will be a waste."

McKenzie looked at her, clearly confused. "What do you mean?"

"We asked our families to come to Wyoming because we thought we could solve this case. But we can't, unless we get into that room."

"You don't know that."

Kate plopped down on the edge of a large rock. "I just don't like to disappoint anyone, especially the Camp Club Girls. They're working hard to figure this out. But we need to do our part, too. And digging in the ground isn't enough. We need to get into the secret, hidden places in the quarry to know what really goes on here."

"Kate, don't get discouraged," McKenzie said. "We'll figure out who did this with the Lord's guidance. But we have to have faith. It won't help anything to give up."

"I just knew the girls were going to win," Kate said sadly. "And since we didn't, well, it just makes me a little mad. I guess I have a bad attitude."

Megan walked up and gave Kate a curious look. "Bad attitude? Who has a bad attitude?"

"Me." Kate sighed as she shrugged out of her backpack. "I must be a sore loser."

Megan laughed. "I've seen a few of those over the years so you're certainly not the first, and I'm sure you won't be the last." She paused. "I think about it this way, Kate. You know how fossils are really imprints?"

"Sure." Kate shrugged, not sure what this had to do with anything.

"We leave an imprint on others with our attitude," Megan said. "Good or bad. A little bit of us rubs off on them. So when you react with an attitude to something—

good or bad—it's like you're creating a. . ." She paused and appeared to be thinking about what to say. "Like a fossil on the heart, if that makes any sense."

At once, a feeling of shame washed over Kate.

"I'm so sorry, Megan. I have had a bad attitude today." She turned to McKenzie. "My faith has been a little low. I guess I just don't see how God is going to solve this."

"Honey, if anyone knows how to dig deep, it's the Lord." Megan patted her shoulder then headed off to join the others.

In the distance, lightning flashed and the girls heard a roar of thunder.

"Oh man. Looks like a storm," Kate said. She grabbed her backpack. "Better get back inside. I don't want my stuff to get wet." She pulled off her wristwatch and tucked it into the backpack to keep it safe, just in case rain fell.

"Race you back to the dorm!" Joel hollered out as he ran by.

Kate took off running behind him. If she couldn't beat him at excavating, maybe she could beat him at racing!

Sure enough, she started gaining on him. By the time they reached the building, she was a few feet ahead of him. She finally stopped, huffing and puffing. Joel grinned as he stopped next to her.

"My backpack is heavier," he explained with a sly wink. "Must be all of those fossils I found today."

Kate and McKenzie groaned.

"I'm just kidding." Joel flashed a smile. "Just a little friendly competition, girls. But seriously, I'm really proud of you. . .especially you, Kate. I understand you found the first *Knightia*. Excavating must come naturally to you."

"I'm not sure it does," she said. "But I did have a lot of fun." She thought about that as they headed into the cabin to get cleaned up. So what if they didn't win? She had learned a lot—about fossils and about her heart.

Curiosity Kicks In

A flash of lightning lit the skies as the girls entered their cabin.

Kate shivered. "Looks like we ended our treasure hunt just in time."

Patti shook her head. "I don't like storms. I hope it doesn't. . ." Just then a loud peal of thunder shook the building. Her lips quivered as she said, "Th—thunder!"

"The storms up here can get pretty intense," Megan said. "So stay indoors."

"Do we have time to shower before lunch?" Kate asked. "I'm sticky and sweaty."

"Me, too," Lauren said. "I've got to get into clean clothes."

"You have plenty of time," Megan said. "Go ahead and shower, then let's sit and talk awhile before lunch. We have plenty of time, and I want to get to know you girls better."

As Kate grabbed clean clothes, she noticed a text message on her phone.

"Who's it from?" McKenzie asked, drawing near.

"Looks like it's from Sydney." She pressed a couple of

buttons and read the message. "Oooh, look, McKenzie."

"Located the missing stingray fossil at a museum in Vancouver." Kate read the words then looked at McKenzie, stunned. "Joel's missing fossil is in Vancouver, Canada? What's it doing there?"

McKenzie shrugged. "I don't know. Maybe the people at Stone's Throw are loaning it to them. Probably isn't any big deal."

Kate shook her head. "Then why doesn't Mr. Jenkins know about it? He owns this place." She lowered her voice. "Unless—he's behind all of this."

She glanced at Megan and thought about how sad the counselor would be to find out her father was a bad guy!

"I don't know, Kate," McKenzie whispered. "I still suspect Grumpy Gus. That makes more sense to me, especially since we saw him with the brown sugar."

"Maybe. But I'm going to ask Sydney to check on one more thing. I need to know how long that stingray fossil has been there, and I need to make sure it's the real deal. Maybe that fossil in Vancouver is a fake, just like the one in Philadelphia."

"So if the one in Vancouver is fake, then where's the real one?"

"Hmm." Kate bit her lip. "I think there's an underground ring of thieves. Maybe Grumpy Gus is just one of many. And maybe. . ." She snapped her fingers as an idea came to her. "Maybe he hasn't had time to sell that one yet. He could be hiding it here somewhere. Maybe that's what he was doing in the woods yesterday, finding the perfect place to hide it."

McKenzie shrugged. "I guess that's possible."

Kate began to pace the room. "If only we'd won the treasure hunt! Then we could have gone into the shipping room instead of the boys. I would have looked for brown sugar. . .or something else to incriminate Grumpy Gus."

McKenzie sighed. "This really stinks. We're getting close to solving the case and can't even get into the room where the forgeries are taking place."

"Maybe we can." Kate chewed on her fingernail, deep in thought.

"What do you mean?"

Kate lowered her voice. "Tonight, after everyone goes to bed, we can go to the shipping room and look around. I'll take my fingerprinting kit and see if there are any prints I can lift."

McKenzie's eyes grew wide. "What if we get caught?"

"We won't. I have an idea. I'll take my little video camera in there, too. I'll find a place to leave it so that we can record Gus. Then we'll have the proof." She looked at McKenzie as a peal of thunder cracked overhead. "You know," she whispered, "there's really only one way we're ever going to solve this."

"Ooh?"

"Yes." She leaned in close and whispered, "If we do make

it into that room, we'll do some serious digging. We need to know if the fossils they're sending out are the real thing or if they're made out of sugar."

"But how do we get in there?" McKenzie whispered.

"I noticed there's a back door leading to that room, too. And when we came across the parking lot after the treasure hunt, that door was propped open with a large stone. Maybe it still is."

McKenzie shook her head. "I don't know, Kate. I want to pray about this while I take my shower."

Kate thought about the case as she showered and she prayed, too. The last thing she wanted to do was to falsely accuse someone. But with the clock ticking away, the girls had very little time to solve this case. Desperate times called for desperate measures. That's what Kate's mom always said anyway.

But how desperate? Should they really sneak out of the cabin and try to enter the prep room? Something about that felt wrong and even a little scary. However, the idea of not solving the case felt even more wrong.

By the time she ended her shower, Kate had talked herself into it. Tonight, while everyone else was asleep, she would take her fingerprint kit, her video camera, and several other gadgets, and she would go into the prep room. . .to see what she could see. Hopefully it would help solve the case.

After showering the girls dressed for lunch. Megan

gestured for them to sit on her bed.

"I just wanted to say something, campers," she said with a smile. "I see a lot of campers come through here and you girls are great! I hate to play favorites, but I'm so happy to be your counselor this week."

Kate reached to hug her. "We're happy to be here. And thank you so much for being a great counselor, Megan."

"It's easy when your campers are as good as mine are." Megan winked and they all smiled.

Soon the campers were sitting in Conner's class on the various types of fossils. Then, as the evening wore into the night, Kate couldn't stop wondering what Grumpy Gus was up to in that back room. With her curiosity getting the better of her, she knew there was only one way to find out. She had to get inside that room, no matter what!

Night Crawlers

"Shh!" Kate used the tiny flashlight on the end of her ink pen to guide the way across the dark quarry parking lot toward the main building. Every step made her a little more nervous than the one before. What were they thinking. . . coming outside in the middle of the night? What would Megan say if she caught them?

Still, they didn't have any other choice, did they? Fossil camp ended tomorrow. If they didn't locate a few more clues tonight, there might not be enough time tomorrow to really figure things out. And Kate couldn't bear the thought of leaving without knowing who forged the fossils. So in spite of her fears, they headed toward the main building. Hopefully, they would make it inside without getting caught. Thank goodness the storm had passed!

"I'm trying to be quiet," McKenzie whispered, "but I just tripped over a rock and it scared me. Everything about being out here scares me. Aren't you frightened?"

"'I can do all things through Christ who strengthens me!'" Kate said. "That's the scripture Elizabeth gave me and

I'm just going to keep saying it!"

"'I can do all things through Christ which strength-eneth me,'" McKenzie repeated several times in a row.

"Not so loud!" Kate whispered. "Someone might hear us."

A coyote's howl stopped them in their tracks.

"D–did you h–hear that?" McKenzie asked.

Kate nodded but kept walking. "Yes. But we can't stop now. C'mon. We're almost at the building."

When they reached the back of the main building, she stopped at the door, praying it was still propped open.

"Oooh, great news!" she whispered, pointing to it. "Let's go inside."

McKenzie took hold of her arm. "Kate, are you sure? If the door's open that probably means someone is inside."

Kate nodded, hoping to convince herself. As she opened the door, it creaked. The girls tiptoed inside, and their eyes adjusted to the dim lighting. The girls realized they were in a tiny enclosed hallway. At the end of the hallway, they saw another door with a see-through glass window in it.

On the other side of the glass, they glimpsed someone moving. A man. The room was dimly lit, so they couldn't tell who it was. Kate ducked and grabbed McKenzie's arm, pulling her down, too. Kate reached into her bag and grabbed her digital camera.

"If you take pictures through the glass, he'll see you," McKenzie whispered.

"I won't stand up to take the pictures. . .and I'll turn off the flash so he won't see anything. Watch and see." Still kneeling, Kate lifted the camera to the bottom of the glass window. "Say a little prayer, McKenzie."

"Trust me, I've been praying ever since we left our cabin."

Kate snapped several photographs, holding the camera at different angles.

"Now what?" McKenzie asked.

"Now we look at the pictures." She quickly scrolled through the pictures she'd just taken. Several weren't very good. But a couple of them showed a large fossil plate.

"Yep, that's him all right," Kate whispered. "I wish I could zoom in the photo to see if that fossil plate is real or not."

"Can we do that on your computer?" McKenzie asked.

"Yes, but I don't want to go back to the cabin just yet." She patted her backpack. "I brought my fingerprint kit. I need to get inside to lift some prints and see if they match the ones on the fossil plate in Philadelphia."

"How can we get in there with someone working?" McKenzie whispered. "It's impossible."

"Maybe he—or she—will leave. You could distract him and I'll go inside."

"Distract him?" McKenzie asked. "H–how?"

"Go to the window on the other side of the room and tap on it. He'll go to the window and I'll slip in and do my work."

"Kate, that's scary." McKenzie paused, and then said, "Okay, okay. I'll do it. But I'm not happy about it."

She slipped out of the back door into the darkness. Kate peeked through the glass pane into the room where the man worked in the shadows. After a few moments, she heard McKenzie tapping on the window and saw the man look up from his work. Unfortunately, he didn't head toward the window. . .he came toward the door!

Kate ran into the parking lot. She called out to McKenzie and soon the two of them were standing in silence on the back of the building in complete darkness. Her heart pounded so loudly she could hear it in her ears. Still, they hadn't gotten caught. That was good.

"Why is it suddenly so dark out here?" McKenzie whispered.

"Someone turned out the light," Kate responded. "Maybe he's trying to spook us."

"Well, it's working!"

The girls stood frozen in their tracks. After a while, they heard a sound at the back door and realized the man—whoever he was—had gone back inside.

"I guess we're safe," McKenzie said with a sigh. "But I'm all turned around now that it's so dark out here. What about you?"

"Yeah, me, too." Kate took a couple of steps to her left. "I think our dorm is this way," she whispered. "Isn't that right?"

"I'm not sure."

They took a couple of steps together and crashed into a trash can. Kate held her breath, hoping no one would notice.

"I don't think we're going the right way," McKenzie whispered. "How will we ever find our way back to the dorm now, Kate?"

"Hmm." Kate paused. "Oh, I know! I have a GPS tracking system on my phone. It's really detailed, so I think it will guide us." She turned it on and within minutes they were headed the right way. Though they bumped into a few things on the way to the cabin, the girls finally made it back safely.

"I don't ever want to be scared like that again!" Kate whispered as they entered the cabin.

The girls tiptoed to their bunks, careful not to wake the others. Kate bumped her toe on the edge of the bed and almost yelped, but stopped herself. If only she could stop her hands from shaking and her knees from knocking!

After fetching her laptop and a bag of chips, she gestured for McKenzie to meet her in the bathroom. There, she plugged her camera into her laptop and downloaded the photos. She opened a photo of a fossil plate.

"That's what I wanted to see," she whispered. "That plate."

She zoomed in. . .close. . .closer. . .closer. . .until she finally got a good look at the fossil plate.

"Hmm." McKenzie shook her head. "When you zoom in on it, it doesn't look like the others in the museum."

"No kidding." Kate opened her bag of chips. "But it looks just like the one I spilled water on that day I was with my teacher. Look here." She searched her computer until she found the copies of the photos she'd taken with her camera that day at the museum. She placed the photos side by side. Sure enough, they looked alike!

"The fossils Grumpy Gus is shipping *are* fakes, just as we suspected," Kate said, taking a bite of a salty chip. "No doubt about that. And I'd guess they're made out of brown sugar, just like these." She pointed to the photo of the ruined fossil plate.

"So it's true." McKenzie bit her lip. "He's shipping fakes. But how do we know he made them, or even knows they're fake?"

"Ooo, look at this one!" She pointed to a picture that showed a man's legs. A man wearing blue jeans. "Does Gus wear jeans? I can't remember."

McKenzie shrugged. "I don't know. I never paid attention."

"I wish we could've gotten in the room so I could've gotten those fingerprints." Kate sighed, and pressed a couple more chips in her mouth.

"Maybe we can do that tomorrow." McKenzie yawned. "But can we talk about this in the morning, Kate? It's really late and I'm so tired."

"What in the world are you girls doing up in the middle of the night?"

Kate looked sheepishly at Megan. "Oh, we, um. . ."

Megan knelt beside her and looked at the computer screen. "And what were you talking about? You found out something about the fake fossils?"

"Sort of." Kate's heart began to thump. She wanted to

tell Megan everything. . .but could she trust her? It was getting harder to know who to trust.

"We have some pictures of someone packing fake fossils to be shipped out," she explained. "We're not sure who it is, but we're sure the fossils are forged. They look just like the brown sugar ones my teacher and I discovered back home in Philly."

"And where did you get these photos?"

"Well, we. . .um. . ." McKenzie's gaze shifted to the ground.

"From the cleaning and shipping room," Kate explained. "I took the pictures."

Megan's brow wrinkled. "Surely you weren't really outside in the middle of the night."

"Well, we, um. . ." Kate sighed.

"Look, I'm all for crime solving," Megan said. "But remember the one rule I told you not to break? You're *not* to go off by yourself. It's too dangerous. And to go off by yourself at night makes it even more dangerous. We have coyotes here."

"I know." A shiver ran down Kate's spine. "We heard them."

"Well you're very fortunate to be back in one piece," Megan said. "But you broke a quarry rule, and I'm really disappointed in you."

Kate's eyes filled with tears right away. "I'm sorry, Megan. And I'm sorry about going outside, too. It was a little scary, being out there all alone. We should have asked you to come with us, but I didn't really want anyone to know what we were doing until we had the proof."

"And this is your proof?" Megan asked, pointing to the computer screen. "Pictures of someone packing fossils?" She examined the photo again. "I'm not even sure who that is, to be honest."

"Don't you see?" Kate said. "We know the fossils are forged. And we know Gus is the one who usually packs them. Doesn't that make him guilty?"

Megan shook her head and rubbed her eyes. "I don't like to accuse anyone without proof. And if I'm going to accuse anyone of anything tonight, it's going to be you two. You broke the rules. I have no choice but to tell Conner and my dad and let them decide if you should be reprimanded or not."

"R—reprimanded?" Kate's eyes filled with tears. "Really?"

"Well, yes. There are always consequences for our actions, Kate. You broke the rules."

"I—I suppose so." She began to cry. "I've never done anything like this before, Megan. I'm so sorry. But we have to figure this out by tomorrow because my teacher is going to lose her job."

"You can't fix everything for everyone, Kate," Megan said. "Some cases aren't yours to solve."

Some cases aren't yours to solve.

Kate dropped into bed, Megan's words tumbling in her head. Maybe her counselor was right. Maybe she *wasn't* supposed to solve this.

But if she wasn't, why did she feel as if she was?

She squeezed her eyes shut, but kept hearing the sound of the coyotes howling, which caused her to tremble all over again!

With images of a man in blue jeans still floating through her brain, Kate finally fell into a troubled sleep.

Digging Deeper

Early the next morning Kate got a phone call from Sydney. Still half-asleep, she answered. "H–hello?"

"Kate, you won't believe it!"

"What is it, Sydney?"

"I called that museum in Vancouver," Sydney explained. "Well actually, my mom called for me. She told them our suspicions about the stingray fossil and guess what?"

"The one they have on display is a fake?" Kate asked.

"That's right. It's a fake!" Sydney squealed. "So the real one is still out there. . .somewhere. Oh, and guess what?"

"What?"

"When we asked them who authorized the fossil to come to them, they didn't have a name. They just said it was a man from Stone's Throw Quarry who set the whole thing up."

Kate sighed. "Well, that could be anyone."

"I know. But we're getting close, Kate. I can feel it!"

"All I feel"—Kate let out a long yawn—"is tired! But thanks for calling, Sydney. This is our last day, so we have to figure this out right away!"

They ended the call and Kate took a shower. Then she and McKenzie searched for Joel. They found him in the dining hall, eating breakfast alone. Most of the others weren't awake yet.

Plopping down at the table, Kate said, "I need to talk to you." She eyed one of his doughnuts, which he gave to her. She popped it into her mouth, enjoying the gooey sweetness. "Yum."

"What do you need to talk about?" Joel looked curious and pressed another doughnut into his mouth.

"We have some news for you." McKenzie sat on the other side of him.

Kate told him all about Sydney's call—every last detail. The more she talked, the more upset Joel got.

"Wait." He stood and began to pace the room. "You're saying that not only is my stingray missing, someone has forged it and sent the forgery to a museum in Canada?"

"That's right." Kate nodded, feeling a lump rise up in her throat. "But stay calm, Joel."

"How can I stay calm? I'm never going to get the internship now. Maybe Mr. Jenkins will think I faked the fossil myself. Maybe he'll think I'm behind this."

"No one will suspect you," McKenzie said.

Kate paused. "Well that's not completely true. I actually suspected him."

"W—what?" Joel said.

She told him about Mrs. Smith's forged fossil and he stared at her, his eyes narrowing.

"You thought I had something to do with that, Kate? You think I would forge fossils and sell them?"

"Well, I. . ." She shook her head. "Oh, I don't know, Joel. I was confused. You have access to the room where this is taking place. And you have motive."

"I—I do?" He looked confused.

"Well sure," Kate said. "You're trying to get that internship. I thought maybe you would do *anything* to get it."

He raked his fingers through his hair and then stared at them once again. "I'd do almost anything to win the internship, but not that. I wouldn't stoop to illegal activity. Besides, I love the Jenkins family. I would never put the quarry at risk. Never." His voice shook with emotion, and Kate suddenly felt awful for accusing him in the first place.

"Let's just forget I said anything about it, okay?" Kate said. "Will you forgive me for suspecting you?"

"Well sure," he said. "But if *you* suspect me, maybe others do, too."

Megan walked into the room just then. "What are you kids talking about? You look pretty intense."

"Megan, we're getting more clues about the fake fossils," Kate explained. "And I'm more curious than ever about who is doing this. We found out that Joel's stingray fossil, which turned up at a museum in Vancouver, was also forged, just like the ones at the museum in Philly."

"Oh no." Megan sat down. "I wonder if my dad knows." She shook her head. "If we don't get this straightened out, our quarry will have a bad reputation. We can't risk that. People all over the country love us, and we want them to know they can trust us."

"There's really only one way," Joel said. "We have to figure this out. . .and fast!"

"Yes, camp ends this afternoon," Kate reminded them. "So we have to work super fast."

"I'll tell you what. . ." Megan shook her head. "I probably shouldn't do this, but I'll help you kids figure this out. I'll do it to help my dad. . .and you."

"That's awesome, Megan," Kate said. "But how?"

"Easy. We'll walk straight into the clean and prep room and see for ourselves. I'll take you there, but we'll have to wait until late this afternoon while the others are at the excavation site."

"We. . .all four of us?" McKenzie asked.

"Well sure. All you had to do was ask," Megan said. "I would have taken you there all along."

Kate slapped herself in the head. "I don't believe it. You're so great, Megan. I thought you would be mad at us after last night."

"What did you do last night?" Joel asked.

Kate filled him in and his eyes grew wide. "You went outside in the dark? With all the coyotes hanging around?"

"Y—yeah," McKenzie agreed. "We didn't know about the

coyotes or we wouldn't have gone."

"We think we'll figure this out once we get in the room," Kate said. "Is it okay to bring my camera and some of my other gadgets?"

"Sure." Megan shrugged. "I don't see why not." She paused a moment, then looked at the girls. "Can I ask you a question?"

"Yes." McKenzie and Kate both spoke at the same time.

"Do you think Gus is the one doing this?"

Kate shrugged. "Maybe."

The wrinkle in Megan's brow grew deeper. "Well, before you judge him too harshly, I think you kids need to know something about him."

"O–okay." Kate gave her a curious look.

"Here's the deal," Megan said. "About two years ago when my dad first met Gus, we fell in love with him. . .and his wife, Jeannie. She was bubbly and fun and always made us laugh."

"I didn't know Gus was married," Joel said. "I've never met his wife."

Megan paused. "Gus and Jeannie were on a road trip to Colorado, carrying some expensive fossils from the quarry where he used to work. Gus was driving the car at the time, and they had a terrible accident late at night."

Kate gasped. "Really? What happened?"

"A driver fell asleep at the wheel and hit Gus's car. Jeannie was badly hurt."

"Oh Megan, that's awful!" Kate said.

"Yes. She spent a long time in the hospital—several months. She's been in a rehab facility ever since. Gus goes to see her every day. I understand the hospital is very expensive."

Kate looked at McKenzie and mouthed the word, "Wow!" Maybe Gus forged the fossils and sold them to make the money he needed for his wife's care.

"On top of all this, the quarry he used to work for fired him because the fossils he was delivering were ruined in the accident."

"That doesn't seem fair," McKenzie said. "Why would they fire him when the accident wasn't his fault?"

"I don't know." Megan shook her head. "But my father felt sorry for Gus and gave him the job here. And even though he's kind of grumpy, we love him very much. He's like a grandfather to me."

Megan started to go on but got distracted by the other campers entering the dining room. Megan headed off in search of Conner.

After she left, Kate turned to McKenzie and Joel. "What did you think of that?"

"Megan obviously thinks Gus is innocent," McKenzie said. "She feels sorry for him because of what happened. I don't blame her. It's a sad story."

"Yes, but. . ."

Joel's eyes narrowed. "I think there's more to the story than meets the eye."

"He has motive," Kate said. "And he obviously needs money."

"Exactly." McKenzie nodded.

"And he does work in that room all alone." Kate's tummy rumbled. "I guess we can talk more about this over some food. I'm so busy solving mysteries that I don't have time to eat. That's inexcusable!"

They all laughed.

After breakfast, the campers headed across the parking lot. Kate saw Gus entering the back door of the building. Something about seeing him troubled her, but she couldn't put her finger on it. It was probably the story Megan had told about what had happened to his wife.

Watch out, Kate, she scolded herself. *Don't start feeling sorry for him!*

Still, something about seeing him today put things in a new light. She pondered that for a minute, trying to make sense of her feelings.

Suddenly Kate snapped her fingers as she realized what had been bothering her so much. "McKenzie!"

"What?"

"Did you see Gus just now?"

"Sure." McKenzie shrugged. "What about him?"

"Did you notice what he was wearing?"

McKenzie's eyes grew wide. "Now that you mention it, yes. He was wearing the quarry uniform—brown pants and a tan shirt."

"*Not* blue jeans," Kate said. "The person in the picture I took last night was definitely wearing jeans."

"Yes, but that picture was taken in the middle of the night," McKenzie said. "So he probably doesn't wear his uniform when he goes to the quarry in the middle of the night to pack the forged fossils. In fact, it's more likely he would wear regular clothes if he's doing something sneaky."

"I suppose." Just one more thing for Kate to think about. But with so little time left, her thoughts were now tumbling around in her head faster than she could keep up with them. If she and McKenzie ever needed prayer. . .now was the time!

The Plot Thickens

Just after breakfast, when the others went to watch a video on the quarry's history, Megan led the way to the prep room. "It's quiet in here during this time of day. Gus does most of his work during the afternoon."

"And in the middle of the night," Kate added.

"The middle of the night?" Megan looked at her curiously. "Are you saying that because you think it was Gus in the pictures you took last night?"

Kate nodded. "Yes."

"Well we don't know that for sure," Megan said. "And remember the story I told you about Gus. We need to assume he is innocent until proven guilty."

"Okay." Kate sighed. Still, she would prove once and for all that Gus did this. Maybe. "Megan, do you mind if I use my fingerprint kit?" Kate asked when they were inside the room.

Megan shrugged. "I don't mind. But remember, Kate, lots of people come in and out of this room, not just Gus. So any prints you lift might belong to other people."

Kate nodded. "I know. I just need to compare the prints to the ones on the fossil plate back in Philadelphia."

She reached in her backpack, pulled out the fingerprint kit and went to work. "Oooh, this is the perfect spot!" She pressed the fingerprint tape down on the table and lifted a perfect print. Kate could hardly wait to compare it to the ones from the ruined fossil back in Philly.

"Here's another one, Kate." McKenzie pointed to a shipping label on a wooden crate. "Might as well get it, too!"

They spent the next five minutes lifting all sorts of fingerprints. Megan watched at the door, in case anyone decided to come in the room.

Just as Kate finished with the last print, she heard a familiar voice.

"What are you girls doing in here?"

Conner. Hopefully he wouldn't be too upset that Megan had let them in the room.

Megan flashed a smile. "Oh hey, Conner. What are you doing here? Aren't you supposed to be with the kids?"

"I had something to take care of first." He looked at her curiously. "Aren't these girls supposed to be watching the video, too?"

"I'll send them in there when we're done," Megan said with a nod. "Something came up and I needed to. . ."

"Needed to what?" He drew near, a concerned look on his face.

"Well I offered to help the girls with something."

Kate tucked the fingerprint kit into her backpack. No point in saying too much.

Just then, the door to the room opened and Grumpy Gus stepped inside. Kate's breath caught in her throat. *Oh no! Caught!*

"What's going on in here, a party?" he asked. "You people filling my workspace for some reason?"

"Well actually, we were. . ." Megan stopped before finishing her sentence.

"She's giving us a tour," Kate said.

"You know how I feel about kids in my work space." Gus looked grumpier than ever. "I don't like them in here."

"Yes, get these campers out of here, Megan," Conner said. He gave her a warning look but Kate still had a couple of questions that needed to be answered, so she jumped right in.

"Can I ask you a question?" She drew near Conner. "What happened to Joel's stingray fossil? It's disappeared from the museum."

"It has not," he said with the wave of a hand. "I had a request from a museum in Vancouver, so I asked Gus to send it."

"I packed it up a week ago and shipped it," Gus said. "Why are you asking?"

"Oh, no reason." Kate shrugged and tried to look calm, though her insides were trembling. She didn't mention that the fossil in Vancouver was a fake.

"You kids get on out of here," Gus said. "I have work to do and I can't do it with you underfoot."

As he shooed them out of the room, Kate had a brilliant idea. She deliberately left her backpack sitting on the floor next to the lab table. Following Megan out of the back door, she tried to still her shaking hands. She whispered the verse that Elizabeth had given her—the one about being able to do all things through Christ who strengthened her—and took a deep breath.

They stepped out into the bright sunlight and Kate planned her next words. She started with two simple ones: "Oh dear."

"What is it, Kate?" Megan looked her way.

"I, um, I left something in the room."

"What?" Megan asked.

"My backpack," she said. "I left it. It'll only take a minute."

Megan held open the door and Kate ran back inside.

"What are you doing in here, kid?" Gus said, looking her way. "I told you that I have work to do."

"Oh, I know." She flashed a smile. "I just came back to get my backpack. Sorry."

Gus grunted and walked to the other side of the room to lift a packing crate. Kate took advantage of the fact that his back was turned and reached inside her backpack, quickly pulling out the tiny digital recorder. She set it in the corner behind a stack of trays and positioned it to face Gus's worktable.

Oh, I hope this works!

She glanced across the room at Gus, who was now heading her way. "Get on out of here, kid. I don't need you leaving stuff in here for me to trip over."

"Yes, sir." She lifted her backpack to show him that she was ready to leave and he grunted again. She was pretty sure she heard him mutter something about kids always getting in his way, but she didn't take the time to listen. No, she had something else to take care of now. Something very important.

She raced back outside, and approached McKenzie and Megan, now out of breath. "I—I need to go back to the cabin and look at these prints," she said. "Is that okay?"

"Yes. I'll walk you there. Then McKenzie and I will join the others in the video room. What are you thinking, Kate?"

"I need to figure out if the fingerprints match. And then, um. . ." She fiddled with her backpack, growing nervous.

"What?" Megan asked.

"Then I need to figure out a way to get back in the shipping room to fetch my video camera, which I just hid behind some trays."

"Brilliant, Kate!" McKenzie clapped her hands together.

Megan laughed. "Wow. You really have done this case-solving thing before, haven't you?"

Kate nodded. "I have. But this time is a little more nerve-racking!"

They walked back to the cabin together, and then Megan

and McKenzie headed to the video room. Kate pulled out her fingerprint kit and examined the prints she had taken that day at the museum. Then she compared them to the ones she had taken today.

The ones from the lab table were a perfect match. Bingo! So were the ones from the shipping crate. Obviously the same person who packed the crate was the one who had forged the fossils, right?

Hmm. She paused to think about that. Like Megan said, more than one person worked in the shipping room. How would she ever know for sure whose fingerprints these were? She would have to print each person who worked in the room. In fact, she would have to print every person who ever went in that room.

Kate pulled out her cell phone and took several pictures of the fingerprints and sent them by picture message to Alexis. "Maybe her uncle can run these prints and tell us who committed the crime," Kate said to herself.

She put all of the items back in her backpack. Then she leaned back against the pillows and began to pray.

"Lord, if You want me to solve this case, I'm really, really going to need Your help. I know the prints match, but I don't know whose prints they are. Lord, can You show us who did this? Was it Gus? Or was it someone else?"

As she continued to pray, Kate's eyes grew heavy. She drifted off into a hazy sleep. She woke almost an hour later! "Oh no! What have I done?" Just as she scrambled to her feet, her phone rang. She looked at the number, recognizing it right away. Elizabeth.

Kate answered with a quick, "Hello?"

"Kate, I was praying for you this morning," Elizabeth said. "And I felt like I was supposed to call and tell you to be extra careful today. I have the strongest feeling someone is pretending to be something they're not."

"Like that Jacob and Esau story," Kate said. "You know what? I think you're right. I've been wondering about something all morning long." She quickly told Elizabeth her suspicions and her friend agreed to pray. In fact, she decided they should stop to pray, right then and there. Over the phone.

"Lord, You know who did this," Elizabeth prayed. "And You know the truth from a lie. We ask that You give Kate and McKenzie wisdom to know the difference today. Help them solve this case, Lord. Amen!"

"Amen!" Kate echoed.

By the time she hung up the phone, she felt energized to finish what she had started. She would figure out who was Jacob and who was Esau. And when she got it figured out, she'd know exactly who had forged those fossils. . .and why!

CHAPTER 15

Putting the Pieces Together

Kate spent the rest of the morning at the excavation site with Megan and the other campers. Conner didn't come because he had other work to do, so it was a quiet day with the boys and girls working together. No competition this time.

Kate really enjoyed her last day digging for fossils, but her mind was on other things. She couldn't stop thinking about the video camera she'd left in the workroom. And she couldn't stop thinking about Gus's brown pants. Something about all of this left her feeling very confused. Mixed up. In fact, the more she thought about it, the more she wondered if they'd had the wrong person all along.

A thousand thoughts rolled through her brain, but only one really made sense. In fact, the more she thought about it, the more sense it made. But how could she prove it? Only one way. Alexis's uncle would have to prove that the fingerprints belonged to the right person.

"Hey, what's up with you today?" Joel asked, drawing near. "You're really quiet. That's not like you."

"I, um, have a lot on my mind." She happened to notice

he was wearing blue jeans. Then again, so were all of the other boys. And Conner. She remembered seeing him in blue jeans earlier today. Then again, he never seemed to wear the quarry uniform, did he?

When the kids took a break for lunch, Kate saw Mr. Jenkins cross the dining hall. Like most of the others, he wore blue jeans. However, she no longer suspected him. After much thought and prayer, she felt he could be trusted. She rose from her place at the table and met him on the opposite side of the room, away from the other campers.

"Mr. Jenkins, I think I'm getting close to figuring this out, but I need your help one more time."

"Oh?"

"Yes, I'm pretty sure I know who's been forging the fossils, and I think the proof is in the workroom."

"What kind of proof?"

"Hopefully a video of someone doing something suspicious. But we won't know for sure until I look at the video. I was wondering if you'd go retrieve my camera for me. I would like to go back to the cabin to watch it after lunch."

"Of course." He nodded. "Now, where is this camera you've hidden?"

"I hid it behind several trays."

"Very crafty!" He grinned. "Okay. I'll go in there and get the camera, but give me a few minutes. I have to talk to Megan first." He disappeared into the kitchen and was gone several minutes. Then Kate watched him walk across the dining hall toward the workroom. She prayed he would be able to get the camera without anyone noticing.

Sure enough, he came out a few minutes later with a paper lunch sack in his hand.

"I think this is yours," he said, placing the lunch bag on the table.

Kate grinned and whispered, "Thanks."

"What is that?" McKenzie asked, taking the seat next to her. "Did you pack your lunch?"

"Not exactly." She giggled then whispered, "It's my video camera." She looked up as Conner entered the dining hall and sat with the boys. "Come with me to the cabin, McKenzie. We still have a case to solve."

They ran across the parking lot together, straight to their cabin. Once inside, Kate plopped on her bunk. She could hardly wait to watch the video. She tried to click on the camera, but it wouldn't come on.

"Don't tell me!" she groaned. "The battery is dead. I should've thought of that. I left it running for too long."

"Did you bring the charger?" McKenzie asked.

"Yes, but it will take awhile to charge." She scrambled off the bunk and looked through her duffel bag until she found the charger. Plugging it in, she sighed. "Everything seems to be taking so long."

"Remember, patience is a virtue!" McKenzie said. "Good things come to those who wait."

"I'm just not very good at waiting." A few minutes later

she checked the camera and it came on. "Awesome!" With her fingers trembling, she rewound the camera to the beginning.

"Ooo, what is that?" McKenzie asked, pointing at the screen.

"Well you can see the edge of the trays," Kate said. "I hid the camera behind them. So we're not going to be able to see much, but maybe we'll hear something suspicious."

She listened closely as a man's voice rang out.

"That's Gus," she said.

"Who's he talking to?"

"Hmm." Kate listened a bit closer. "Sounds familiar." Another moment later, she recognized the other voice. "Oh, that's Conner."

"Gus is saying something to him, but I can't make it out."

Kate backed up the video and listened closely. Off in the distance, faint as a whisper, she heard Gus say, "Conner, I'm surprised you're still going strong today. Didn't you work through the night?"

McKenzie's eyes grew as wide as saucers. "No way! Conner was the one in the room last night?"

"Sounds like it." Kate's stomach began to get butterflies. This confirmed what she had been thinking all morning. She kept watching and listening to the video, hoping to learn more.

"What is Conner saying?" McKenzie asked. "I can't make it out."

"Sounds like Conner is telling Gus to take a break. Telling him that he will take over for a while."

"Ooo, I think I heard the door close," McKenzie added. "Do you think Gus left the room?"

"Maybe, but look." Kate pointed at the screen. "You can see a man's legs, but I'm not sure whose they are! The picture is fuzzy."

McKenzie squinted and took a closer look. "That has to be Conner. Gus is wearing his uniform today, remember?"

"Oh right!" Kate watched as the man in the blue jeans walked by. For a while the room grew silent. Then she heard Conner speaking again. This time his words were a lot clearer, thank goodness.

"Who is he talking to?" McKenzie asked. "There's no one in the room with him."

"Maybe there is!" Kate whispered. "Maybe someone else came in." She listened closely as Conner said something about fossils.

"Ooo, I know!" McKenzie snapped her fingers. "He's talking to someone on the phone. Has to be, because we can only hear what Conner is saying, not what the other person is saying."

"I think you're right," Kate agreed. "But it's hard to tell what he's talking about."

They listened a little bit longer, and Kate gasped when she heard Conner start to laugh. He said something that sounded like, "We got away with it."

"Did he really just say 'we got away with it'?" McKenzie asked. "Or am I imagining things?"

"That's what I thought he said, too!" Kate nodded. She pushed the rewind button on the video camera and played that part over again. Sure enough, it really sounded like those were his words. She rewound it and played it once more, this time slowing down the speed. "Weeee. . .gooooooooot. . .a. . . way. . .with. . .it." Plain as day!

After that, Conner's words were a little muffled, but the girls could understand part of it, especially when he said, "Meet me in the parking lot at three, but watch out. Some kids are snooping around, so we have to be careful this time."

McKenzie gasped. "Oh Kate!"

After that, the screen went black.

"Must be when the battery died." Kate let out an exaggerated sigh. "But at least we know Conner is up to something here."

"I just don't believe it!" McKenzie looked stunned. "Why Conner? He's got a great job here at the quarry. Paleontologists make a good living. Why would he need to forge the fossils and sell them illegally?"

"I don't know. But I've had a funny feeling all morning that he's our bad guy. He's been pretending to be something—or someone—he's not." Kate filled McKenzie in on Elizabeth's phone call earlier this morning and McKenzie looked stunned.

"Wow."

133

"Yeah," Kate nodded. "So I've been praying all morning that God would reveal the truth, and now I'm pretty sure He has. Just one last thing we have to do. We have to pray that Alex's uncle is able to run the fingerprints through the computer before we leave the camp today. Otherwise we won't be able to prove anything."

"Maybe we can," McKenzie said. "Come with me." She grabbed Kate's hand and ran in the direction of the dining hall. Once inside, she passed the other kids and went into the kitchen. The cook looked over at the girls with a surprised look on his face.

"What's up, kids?"

"I just have a quick question," McKenzie said. "Might sound kind of silly, but has anyone who works at the quarry ever come into the kitchen to borrow any brown sugar?"

"Brown sugar?" The cook shrugged. "Yeah. Why?"

"Do you remember who?"

"Well sure," he said. "Conner. It's the funniest thing. I've never heard of anyone who uses brown sugar in his coffee, but Conner does. He seems to love just nibbling on the stuff, too. So he's always in here looking for sugar."

"Bingo!" Kate yelled. She grabbed McKenzie by the hand and they ran out of the kitchen, hollering "Thank you!" to the cook as they ran.

"What do we do now?" McKenzie asked.

Kate glanced at the clock. "Hmm. It's two o'clock. Dad should be here at three to pick us up."

"That's the same time Conner is going to pass the real fossils off to whoever he was talking to on the phone," McKenzie whispered. "What do we do now?"

"Now we tell Mr. Jenkins," Kate said. "And then he calls the police. Looks like the Camp Club Girls have found their man!"

Biscuit to the Rescue!

Kate and McKenzie found Mr. Jenkins in the dining hall chatting with several campers.

"Could I talk to you again, sir?" Kate asked anxiously.

"Well sure, Kate."

"In your offie?" she said. "And please bring Megan."

"Well sure." He leaned over with a twinkle in his eye. "I have a feeling you're going to share some big news."

"The biggest news ever!" she whispered in response.

Minutes later Mr. Jenkins took a seat at his desk, and Megan sat in a chair nearby. Kate and McKenzie paced the room.

"What is it, Kate?" Megan asked. "You're making me nervous!"

Kate glanced at the clock on the wall—2:10. "We don't have much time. We have to call the police."

"Police?" Megan asked. "Why?"

Kate pointed to Mr. Jenkins's television. "Do you mind if I plug in my video camera so I can show you something?"

"Be my guest."

Seconds later, they were all watching the video together. Dismay filled Megan's voice. "Oh, I don't believe it! Not Conner! He's my friend! I trusted him!"

"Looks like he fooled us." Mr. Jenkins reached for the phone and dialed 911. Kate could hear him talking to the police. She hated to interrupt, but felt it was important.

"Mr. Jenkins, tell them to come a couple of minutes after three. You need to catch him in the act if you want the charges to stick."

"Good idea." He nodded and conveyed his wishes to the police, who agreed to come at five minutes after three.

"What do we do now?" McKenzie asked.

"Conner is teaching the final session in the dining hall," Megan said. "Let's all go back in there and act like nothing is unusual. Just be ourselves."

"This will be the best acting job of my life!" Kate said. She looked at Mr. Jenkins and Megan and said, "But I am sorry that the bad guy turned out to be one of your employees. I'm sure this is really hard to hear."

"It is," Mr. Jenkins said. A puzzled look crossed his face. "I'm so disappointed. I've been mentoring Conner for years. He's like a son to me. It breaks my heart that he would steal from me."

"I just can't believe he was pretending to be something he wasn't all of this time." Megan shook her head and brushed away some tears. "I will never understand that."

Kate thought of the story of Jacob and Esau once again.

How interesting that Conner was a fake, just like the brother in the story!

The girls walked into the dining hall and took their seats at the table. Conner looked at them with a troubled glance as he saw Mr. Jenkins and Megan enter the room behind Kate and McKenzie.

"He's nervous," Kate whispered. "I think he knows something's up."

She listened as he gave his final speech—something about the work paleontologists were doing with fossils around the world—but was distracted when a text message came through on her phone. She tried not to look obvious as she opened the phone, but it was hard! Kate almost swallowed her bubble gum when she read the text from Alexis: KATE, THE PRINTS DON'T BELONG TO GUS. THEY BELONG TO CONNER. HE'S BEEN IN TROUBLE FOR SOME PETTY THEFT BEFORE, SO THE FINGERPRINTS WERE IN THE COMPUTER SYSTEM.

Kate passed the phone to Mr. Jenkins, who sat behind her. He read the words and pursed his lips, then passed the phone back to her.

When the session came to an end at 2:45, the campers were dismissed to load their gear and prepare for their parents' arrivals. Kate grew more excited by the moment. Any time now, the police would be here. And her father. She prayed for God's protection over everyone involved.

At exactly 2:55 she and McKenzie walked to the front

parking lot with Mr. Jenkins and Megan nearby. She smiled as a familiar RV pulled into the parking lot.

"Hey, my dad brought the RV!" McKenzie said. "Cool."

"Perfect to hide behind!" Kate added.

They greeted their family members. Dex looked excited to see them. So did Biscuit, who jumped up and down.

"Be still, boy," Kate said. "We don't have time for you to go crazy right now!"

"Did you have a good time girls?" Kate's father asked.

"Did you figure out who forged the fossils?" Dex added.

"Yes," Kate whispered. "But we can't really talk about it yet." She looked up at her father. "Dad, we need to stay a few more minutes. I promise it won't take too long."

He shrugged. "If it will help you girls out, sure."

Kate looked across the parking lot as an unfamiliar car pulled up. She watched Conner emerge from the trees on the far side of the parking lot with something large in his hand. A briefcase, maybe?

"McKenzie, look!" She reached for her camera and snapped pictures.

"Kate, what in the world is happening?" her mother asked.

"I promise I'll tell you everything!" She kept taking pictures. "But right now we have to wait on the police!"

"The police?" Mrs. Phillips fanned herself.

The man in the car pulled close to Conner and popped open his trunk. At that moment, Mr. Jenkins headed their way. Kate prayed for his protection. When he arrived next to Conner, the men began to argue. Kate watched in horror as Conner ran toward the trees. She glanced at Biscuit and hollered, "Biscuit! Go get him, boy!"

Biscuit the Wonder Dog took off running across the parking lot. He caught up with Conner just as a patrol car pulled into the parking lot, sirens wailing. Biscuit grabbed hold of Conner's jeans with his teeth and held on for dear life.

"Let go of me, you dumb dog!" Conner yelled. He shook his leg and Biscuit bounced a little, but held on tight, yanking this way and that.

Seconds later the police caught up with Conner. One of them patted Biscuit on the head. "Good boy, puppy," he said, scratching him behind the ears.

"His name is Biscuit the Wonder Dog!" Kate called out. "He's a crime-solving dog!" She took a few steps toward the officers, but they gestured for the kids to keep their distance.

"Stay over there," the officer called out. "We'll get statements from you after."

Kate nodded. She knew better than to interrupt a crime scene! Biscuit ran to her and she hugged him.

"Good puppy, Wonder Dog!"

She and McKenzie peeked around the edge of the RV, watching the police arrest Conner. As they did, several of the other campers drew near.

"What in the world is going on?" Lauren asked.

"Yeah, why are the police talking to Conner?" Patti asked.

Joel simply shook his head, a sad look in his eyes. Finally he whispered, "I don't believe it. I really don't believe it. I thought Conner was a great guy."

Kate shrugged. "Even really great people make mistakes."

"And this was a big one!" McKenzie added.

The police now put Conner in the back of the patrol car with the other man and pulled out of the parking lot. Mr. Jenkins walked toward the campers with a sad look on his face.

"You'll never believe what the police just found in Conner's trunk," he said.

"Brown sugar?" McKenzie and Kate spoke in unison.

"Actually, they did find traces of brown sugar, but that's not what I'm talking about," Mr. Jenkins said. "They found the actual stingray fossil and a little black book with phone numbers of the people Conner has been selling the real fossils to. It's an underground ring of fossil thieves."

"I knew it!" Kate turned to McKenzie with a smile. "The Camp Club Girls were right! He was selling the real fossils to make money."

"Have you ever heard of an artist named Jean Van Horn?"

"I have," Megan said, her eyes growing wide. "He's Conner's best friend."

"Well apparently he's been using the real fossils for artwork. It's a common practice, but not one that many people know much about. They take the fossils and turn them into art masterpieces, then sell them for hundreds of thousands of dollars. The stolen fossils are so beautifully disguised when the artist is done with them that they're not even recognizable."

"Wow." Kate shook her head. "That's amazing."

"Thankfully Conner confessed to the officer," Mr. Jenkins said, looking at Kate. "And when I asked him about the fossils that were supposed to be sent to your teacher's museum in Philadelphia, he promised to tell the police where they are."

"Yea!" Kate hollered. "Mrs. Smith's job is saved!"

"Thanks to you girls." He smiled at Kate and McKenzie. "You're the real heroes here."

"Nah." Kate felt her cheeks turn warm with embarrassment.

Mr. Jenkins nodded. "Yes you are! And I should offer a reward for those fossils."

"Oh no, sir!" Kate said. "We didn't do this for a reward. We did it to help you and so my teacher could keep her job at the museum."

"Then at least let me offer you kids some ice cream before you go," he said with a twinkle in his eye. "It's the least I can do!"

All of the campers went back inside the dining hall for ice cream sundaes. As they ate, Megan drew near, still looking a little sad.

"I still can't believe it was Conner. He was my friend." She sighed.

"I'm sure you're really disappointed," McKenzie said.

"I am." She paused. "You know, all of this talk about fake fossils has reminded me of something."

"What's that?" Kate looked her way.

"Well the Bible says we're supposed to let our yes be yes and our no be no. In other words, we're supposed to be who we say we are. No faking it."

"Ah." Kate nodded.

"Just seems like so many people say they're Christians, but don't really act like it. Or maybe sometimes they fake it when they're around their church friends, but when they're at school or hanging out with another crowd, they act differently."

"I know what you mean," McKenzie said. "One of my friends from church is like that. I've tried to talk to her about it, but she still keeps on pretending when she's around the kids at church. I see what she's like at school, and she's really different."

"Maybe there's a lesson to be learned from this fossil fiasco," Megan said with a sigh. "Maybe God is trying to show us that it's so important to be the real deal. Genuine."

Kate nodded. "No fakes!"

"That's right." Megan nodded. "No fakes. You know why? Because it dishonors Him when we pretend to be something we're not. And if we think others won't notice, we're wrong! People are pretty good at spotting fakers."

"That's true," McKenzie said.

Kate noticed Joel standing to the side, very quiet, staring at the ground.

"You okay, Joel?" she asked, drawing near.

He shrugged. "I don't know."

"What do you mean? You know everything!" She gave him a warm smile.

"No I don't." He shook his head. "I mean, I know some things. Scientific things. Things about fossils. But I don't really know what you're talking about."

"What do you mean?"

He shrugged. "I go to church on Sundays with my mom and dad. And I even go to Sunday school. But mostly it's to make my parents happy, or to hang out with friends. I'm not really going for any reason other than that."

"Wow." Kate paused before responding. At least he was being honest about it! "You know what, Joel?" she said at last. "I'm really proud of you. You didn't have to tell me that. You could have just gone on pretending. But you were honest."

"Yeah, I guess so." He took a seat, looking more defeated. "But watching you and McKenzie the past few days has shown me something. You two are the real deal. You really love God. It's obvious."

Kate got a happy tingly feeling all over. "Thank you, Joel."

He paused, then gave her a hopeful look. "I guess what I'm trying to say is, you two aren't fakers, but I am."

"Ah." Kate didn't say anything more. She wanted to give him a chance to finish.

"I don't want to fake it anymore," Joel said.

"Have you ever asked Jesus to live in your heart?"

McKenzie asked, drawing near. "If you give your heart to Him, He will show you how to live a real Christian life, one where you don't have to pretend."

Joel shook his head. "No, I never did that. I just go to church, like I said."

"Well going to church isn't what makes you a Christian," Kate explained. "The only thing that really gives you a real relationship with God is making Jesus Lord of your life. When you do that, everything becomes *very* real, trust me!"

McKenzie nodded. "She's right, Joel. You won't have to fake it anymore."

He gave her a curious look. "So, um, how do I do that?"

"You can pray and ask Jesus to come into your heart," Kate explained.

He shrugged. "I, um. . .well, I don't know how to do that."

Kate smiled, and thought about Elizabeth at once. Elizabeth would say, "Kate, don't ever be afraid to stop what you're doing and pray for someone, even if it's in a public place."

With a happy heart, Kate did just that.

A Fossil on the Heart

After praying with Joel to accept Jesus, Kate felt like singing! She felt like dancing and jumping for joy. Was this how God felt, too? Probably! The angels in heaven were probably throwing a party right now!

Kate's mother drew near. "Honey, I hate to rush you, but we have to get back to Yellowstone soon. Tonight is our last evening with the Phillips family, and we want to have a big campfire and let you and McKenzie tell us the whole story of how you caught the forger."

Kate nodded. "Okay, Mom. I'll be right there. I just need to talk to one last person. Can you give us about five minutes?"

"Sure." Her mother gave her a warm hug. "And in case I haven't said it yet, I'm so proud of you!"

"The Camp Club Girls did it together!" Kate said with a nod.

Her mother headed to the RV, and Kate walked with McKenzie and Joel into the museum, looking for Gus. Kate spotted him at last.

"Gus, could we talk to you for a minute?" she asked.

He shook his head. "I'm busy, kid."

"It will only take a minute. Please?" She looked into his tired eyes and he shrugged.

"I guess. But make it quick."

"I. . .we. . .just wanted to tell you something," Kate explained. "We wanted to tell you how happy we are that you work here. You do a great job for the quarry and we appreciate you."

He stared at her suspiciously. "Who told you to say this?"

"No one," McKenzie said. "We just wanted you to know, that's all."

Gus ran his fingers through his thinning hair and looked at them as if he didn't quite believe them. "You mean, you're just saying this to be nice?"

"Well sure," Kate said. "When someone does a great job, it's always a good idea to let them know."

"If you think I'm so great, then why were you kids snooping around this place at night, hoping to catch me doing something wrong?" he asked. "I know all about it."

"Sorry about that." Kate sighed. "We were just trying to figure out who was making the fake fossils."

"I know, I know." Gus put his hands up. "You thought it was me. But now I have something to tell you."

"Oh?" Kate gave him a curious look. "What is it?"

"I suspected Conner of foul play all along," Gus said. "I've been keeping an eye on him for weeks, documenting suspicious activity."

"No way!" Kate crossed her arms at her chest and stared at him. "Were you in the woods one day when we were excavating? I thought I saw you."

"Yes, I followed him out there that day because I'd found a large bag of brown sugar hidden in the closet in my workroom earlier in the day. I took it to the kitchen, thinking maybe one of our cooks had misplaced it, but they thought I was crazy, so I took it back to the workroom."

"Wow. So that explains why we saw you walk through the dining hall with a bag of brown sugar," Kate said.

"Yes." He sighed. "Something told me Conner was up to no good, but I couldn't prove it. I hated to go to Mr. Jenkins without any proof."

"I see." She paused then looked at him. "Are you saying you knew all along that the fossils you were sending out were fake, but you sent them anyway?"

"No." He laughed. "I only began to suspect it when you kids started following me. I overheard something you said to Mr. Jenkins. Just enough to get me curious. And to be honest, I was worried about Joel's missing stingray, but I hadn't said anything about it."

"Wow. So we were all worried about the same thing," Kate said. "To think we could have been working together!"

"Yep." Gus grinned—the first smile she'd seen from him. "Would you kids like a proper tour of my workroom? A lot of interesting things go on back there."

Kate looked up at him, stunned at his kind gesture. "Really?"

"Really." He nodded and grinned.

"That would be great. We can't take long though, because my parents are waiting."

"They can come, too," Gus said. "Run and fetch them."

Kate did just that, and before long, both families were crammed into the tiny workspace.

As Gus showed them around, he was all smiles. "Wow. He's really great," Kate whispered to McKenzie.

Kate thought about everything that had happened. How she had misjudged people!

The tour ended after just a few minutes, and it was time to leave the quarry. Kate had a hard time saying good-bye to everyone, especially Megan and Joel.

"Promise you'll write?" Joel asked.

"I will. And you let me know if you get that internship."

"Oh, I forgot to tell you! Mr. Jenkins told me this morning that I did!" Joel's faced beamed. "Isn't that terrific news?"

"Awesome!" Kate turned to Megan, feeling tears well up in her eyes. She reached to hug her counselor good-bye and whispered, "I'm going to miss you so much."

"I'm going to miss you, too," Megan said. "And I can never thank you enough for helping solve this case, girls," she said, reaching for McKenzie with her other arm. "I hope you'll come back."

Kate nodded. "Maybe we'll get to come back someday and bring our friends. You'll love Elizabeth. And Sydney and Alex and Bailey. . ." On and on she went, singing the praises of the Camp Club Girls.

Finally Kate's mother interrupted her. "I'm so sorry, honey, but we really have to go."

"Okay." Kate sighed and gave the quarry one last look before they climbed into the RV. As they pulled out of the parking lot, she felt the sting of tears in her eyes but quickly brushed them aside. No tears today. This was a happy day.

"Mom, would it be okay if I called Mrs. Smith?" Kate asked. "I want to tell her what happened."

"Yes, it's fine," her mother said. "I know she'll be very relieved."

Kate spent the next ten minutes on the phone with her teacher, who was thrilled to get the news, especially when she heard that the real fossils had been located and would be sent to the Philadelphia museum in a few days.

"Kate, you did it! You solved the case *and* saved the day."

"I hate to disagree with you, Mrs. Smith," Kate said, "but only God can save the day. I am glad He chose to use the Camp Club Girls to help though!"

"Me, too." Her teacher laughed then thanked her once again for helping out.

Kate ended the call, then looked at McKenzie. "Now we need to call the other girls and let them know what happened!"

"Yes, they'll be so excited!" McKenzie added.

"Awesome! Let's do a conference call."

Minutes later, Kate had all of the Camp Club Girls on

the line. Everyone was so excited that they talked on top of each other.

Kate held the phone in her hand and McKenzie leaned in close to hear everything.

"We have so much to tell you!" Kate said. "We figured out who forged the fossils!"

"No way!" Bailey let out a loud squeal. Kate pulled the phone away from her ear and rubbed it, then laughed.

"Yes. And you're never going to believe who it was. The very last person on planet earth that we would have ever suspected—Conner! Alex already knows because her uncle helped us run the fingerprints, but I wanted to tell the rest of you."

Kate quickly relayed the rest of the story, giving the girls all of the details then thanking each of the girls for her help.

"Oh wow, that's unbelievable!" Sydney said. "Conner seemed so trustworthy."

"I know," Kate said. "He's a respected paleontologist and a counselor to the boys. That's why I never considered him. But in the end, that's who it turned out to be."

"So Gus wasn't the one after all?" Bailey asked.

"No, it looks like we judged a book by its cover. . .and we were wrong," Kate answered.

"What do you mean?" Sydney asked.

"I saw a grumpy older man in wrinkled clothes and thought he was a bad guy. Turns out he's just a man who is hurting. His poor wife is in a rehab hospital because of a terrible car accident. Instead of judging Grumpy Gus, I should have shared God's love with him." Even as she spoke the words, Kate felt guilty.

"Don't let her fool you," McKenzie said. "Kate *did* show him God's love. Every time she passed by, she smiled and talked to him. That's a lot more than most of the other campers did."

It warmed Kate's heart to hear McKenzie's words, but she still felt bad.

"Remember what happened in the story of Jacob and Esau," Elizabeth said. "Even though Jacob made some mistakes, God still made something good out of the situation. That's how the Lord works. You watch and see."

"O—okay. I will."

"I see one good thing that came out of it already," Sydney said. "You suspected the wrong person, but your suspicions led to the right person. Don't you find that interesting?"

"Yes." Kate couldn't help but smile. "I learned a big lesson."

"What's that?" Alexis asked.

"Megan told me on the day of the treasure hunt that we each leave an imprint on others with our attitude. She called it a fossil on the heart."

"Ooo, I like that," Elizabeth said. "A fossil on the heart."

"When my attitude is good, I leave a good imprint and when my attitude is bad, well. . ." Kate paused and sighed. "Let's just say that sometimes I leave a negative imprint."

Sydney laughed. "Kate, don't be so hard on yourself.

You're one of the sweetest girls I know. You've left a great imprint on my heart. And on Bailey's. And Elizabeth's." She began to talk nonstop about how each of the Camp Club Girls had left a different imprint. Before long, Kate was laughing. The Camp Club Girls all started laughing and talking and soon got really loud. Kate's mom gave her a warning look.

Kate ended the call just as they arrived at their campsite at Yellowstone. The sun was starting to set in the west, painting the sky the most brilliant colors Kate had ever seen.

She and the others climbed out of the RV and stretched their legs.

"I'm so hungry!" she said. "What's for dinner?"

"We're grilling hamburgers and hot dogs," her mother said. "You girls can help."

Kate and McKenzie helped their mothers get the meal ready. As they worked, Dexter drew near, his eyes wide with excitement.

"Kate, you'll never believe what happened when you were gone."

"What?" She looked at her little brother.

"Yesterday morning we had a bear. He came right to the edge of our tent."

"No way!"

"It's true," her mother said. "I think someone. . ." she looked at Dexter, "someone left the bag of marshmallows out. And a little bear cub found it at the campsite, just a few feet from our tent."

"I wish you could've seen it, Kate," Dexter said with a grin. "I came out of the tent and caught him in the act."

"What did you do?"

"Well, I read online not to ever spook a bear, so I stayed quiet. For a minute or two he didn't know I was there."

"We watched the whole thing from our tent," her father said. "The cub was so busy eating marshmallows that he wasn't paying attention to anything. But as soon as he saw Dex, he took a couple of steps in his direction."

"Then what?" Kate could hardly believe it.

Dexter shook his head. "I stood frozen like a statue."

"We all prayed silently," her mother said. "The Lord answered our prayers. The bear ate that last marshmallow and then took off into the trees."

"When he left we ran and got inside the van," Dexter said. "Just in case he came back."

Kate's father said, "He didn't come back. He went off, probably looking for more food."

"I'm so glad I didn't go to fossil camp with you," Dexter said. "I would have missed the whole thing."

"See!" Kate laughed. "I told you God had an adventure in store for you."

When everyone gathered around the campfire with food, between mouthfuls of their yummy burgers, Kate and McKenzie told them the whole story. Afterward, one thing stood out above all the others. Kate still heard Megan's words echoing in her ears. . ."*We leave an imprint on others with our attitude. A little bit of us rubs off on them. So, when you react with an attitude to something—good or bad—it's like you're creating a fossil on the heart.*"

"A fossil on the heart," Kate whispered once again.

This was *one* lesson she knew she would never forget.

Join the Camp Club Girls online!

www.campclubgirls.com

✿ Get to know your favorite Camp Club Girl in the Featured Character section.

✻ Print your own bookmarks to use in your favorite Camp Club Book!

✻ Get the scoop on upcoming adventures!

(Make sure to ask your mom and dad first!)

Follow the Camp Club Girls

IN ALL THEIR ADVENTURES!

Book 9: Alexis and the
Arizona Escapade
ISBN 978-1-60260-292-2

Book 10: Kate's Vermont Venture
ISBN 978-1-60260-293-9

Book 11: McKenzie's Oregon
Operation
ISBN 978-1-60260-294-6

Book 12: Bailey's Estes
Park Excitement
ISBN 978-1-60260-295-3

Book 13: Elizabeth's San Antonio
Sleuthing
ISBN 978-1-60260-402-5

Book 14: Sydney and the
Wisconsin Whispering Woods
ISBN 978-1-60260-403-2

Book 15: Bailey and the
Santa Fe Secret
ISBN 978-1-60260-404-9

Available wherever books are sold.